THE BODY IN THE WATER

I stood on the end of the dock, gazing at the river. Sleek sailboats bobbed at their moorings. The oyster cages moved gently with the current. On a small island, an eagle sat in a nest at the top of a pine tree. Houses peeked out here and there among green treetops. Across the river, Ken Farrow was out on his dock, readying his boat as if to go out. Red stood watching, his long tail occasionally fluttering in anticipation of the ride. At my aunt and uncle's dock, *My Sharona* was gone. Uncle Bob was probably farther down the river, closer to the sea, dropping his lobster traps into position, getting ready for the season.

It was all so quiet and peaceful.

I don't know what made me look down.

It took me a moment to comprehend what I was looking at. Then I did. Andie's body bobbed in the water at the end of the dock, looking as peaceful as the rest of the scene . . .

Books by Barbara Ross

Maine Clambake Mysteries
CLAMMED UP
BOILED OVER
MUSSELED OUT
FOGGED INN
ICED UNDER
STOWED AWAY
STEAMED OPEN
SEALED OFF
SHUCKED APART

Collections
EGG NOG MURDER
(with Leslie Meier and Lee Hollis)
YULE LOG MURDER
(with Leslie Meier and Lee Hollis)
HAUNTED HOUSE MURDER
(with Leslie Meier and Lee Hollis)

Jane Darrowfield Mysteries
JANE DARROWFIELD, PROFESSIONAL
BUSYBODY
JANE DARROWFIELD AND THE MADWOMAN
NEXT DOOR

Published by Kensington Publishing Corp.

Shucked Apart

Barbara Ross

KENSINGTON
PUBLISHING CORP.

www.kensingtonbooks.com

KENSINGTON BOOKS are published by

Kensington Publishing Corp.
119 West 40th Street
New York, NY 10018

All Kensington titles, imprints, and distributed lines are available at special quantity discounts for bulk purchases for sales promotion, premiums, fund-raising, educational, or institutional use.

Special book excerpts or customized printings can also be created to fit specific needs. For details, write or phone the office of the Kensington Sales Manager: Attn.: Sales Department. Kensington Publishing Corp., 119 West 40th Street, New York, NY 10018. Phone: 1-800-221-2647.

The Kensington logo is a trademark of Kensington Publishing Corp.

First Printing: March 2021
ISBN-13: 978-1-4967-1796-2
ISBN-10: 1-4967-1796-1

ISBN-13: 978-1-4967-1799-3 (ebook)
ISBN-10: 1-4967-1799-6 (ebook)

10 9 8 7 6 5 4 3 2 1

Printed in the United States of America

To Sylvie Marie Donius, who arrived with a smile that lights up the darkness at the moment we needed it most.

CHAPTER ONE

"Julia, meet my friend Andie." My boyfriend Chris, looking tousled and handsome as always, stood in the doorway of my office. He entered the room, confident and casual, and a pleasant-looking woman followed.

"You mean Andie from your poker nights?" I put my hand out to cover my confusion. For two years, I'd been laboring under the misapprehension that "Andy" was a man. "No, we haven't. I'm Julia."

She took my hand and shook. "Andie. Greatorex. So glad to *finally* meet." Her handshake was firm and strong, which seemed right given her looks. She was tall, broad-shouldered, and obviously fit. Her sandy-blonde hair, pulled back in a high ponytail, framed a round face with wide set, hazel eyes. She appeared to be in her mid-thirties, like Chris and me. Also, like Chris and me, she wore jeans, work boots, a T-shirt and a plaid, flannel overshirt, as if we were planning on starting our own Grunge band. Andie's T-shirt was maroon and had the words, GREAT RIVER OYSTERS on it in white block letters. My T-shirt was navy and said, SNOWDEN FAMILY CLAMBAKE. Chris "doesn't wear advertising," quote, unquote, so his T-shirt was blank.

In other words, we were dressed appropriately for a morning in coastal Maine in mid-May. Outside, pre-season tourists From Away wore jackets and windbreakers, but we natives were hardier.

I looked from Chris to Andie and back again, wondering why they were here. It could have been an informal visit, Chris running into Andie on the street and spontaneously deciding to bring her to meet me in the second-floor office in my mother's house where I ran our clambake business. Somehow, I doubted it.

He took a step forward and spoke. "I invited Andie today because she has a problem and we wondered if you could help."

I was intrigued. "Please sit." They sat in the two wooden guest chairs on the other side of the big mahogany desk that had been my late father's when he ran the business. The office was large and light. Three windows across the front of the house allowed me to look down the hill to the town pier, where our ticket kiosk stood and where our tour boat, the *Jacquie II*, was docked waiting for customers who would start coming Memorial Day Weekend. I hadn't changed a thing about the room since my dad had died. It still had the metal file cabinets in the corner and the big prints of sailing ships on the walls.

"How can I help?" I asked.

Andie glanced at Chris for encouragement and then began. "I was robbed yesterday."

"That's terrible." Busman's Harbor was a place where people left keys in their vehicles and the doors to their homes unlocked. But we weren't immune from the scourge of drug addiction that plagued the rest of the country and the petty theft that went with it.

"She was attacked and then robbed," Chris clarified.

That was different, and far, far more unusual. "How awful. I am so sorry." I looked into Andie's lightly freckled face. She didn't seem the worse for wear, no scratches or bruises. I felt badly for her, but I didn't see what it had to do with me.

Andie cleared her throat. "Chris has talked at poker, many times, about how you've helped the police solve crimes. He's proud of you." She smiled at Chris who beamed at me. He wasn't one to parade his feelings around, and I felt a warm glow creeping up my neck into my face. Where was this going? "And when this happened, I thought, well, I thought maybe you could help. So I called Chris, and here we are."

Questions and more questions. "What was stolen?" I expected an answer like cash, credit cards, phone.

"Two buckets of oyster spat."

"What the what?" *Spat?*

Andie smiled and her shoulders dropped into a more relaxed position. "Two big white pails of oyster seed— teeny-tiny baby oysters. I run the Great River Oyster Farm on the Damariscotta River. I bought the seed from the hatchery and was carrying the buckets from my truck to my dock when it happened."

Oyster seed. That was a new one. "Did you report it to police?"

"In Damariscotta, right away." Damariscotta was the largest town on the next peninsula north of ours (or east of ours, as Mainers would have it). The town was about forty minutes from Busman's Harbor at times of the year when there wasn't any tourist-related traffic.

I shifted in my chair, preparing to deliver a difficult message. "I know it seems like twenty-four hours is a long time when you've been assaulted and robbed. I can't imagine how you must be feeling. But you need to give the police more time."

She waved a hand. "I'm not concerned about the time. The oysters are dead unless the person who robbed me has the equipment and know-how to care for them. I'm concerned the police don't understand the motive."

"Don't understand it how?" The motive for most robberies seemed pretty straightforward. You have something the other person wants. End of story.

Andie took a deep breath. "The police think it was a simple robbery." She paused. "I think it was an act designed to cripple my business. Sabotage."

A loaded word. My eyebrows jumped involuntarily. "Sabotage. How, who, and why?"

"That's what I'd like you to help me figure out."

"You think someone is out to get you, but you don't know who or why?"

Andie nodded. "Right. The method was stealing the seed. It doesn't make sense that someone would do it for the money. This was done specifically to hurt me. There's no other explanation for it."

I doodled on the leather-framed paper calendar that functioned as a blotter on my desk, buying time. It was flattering that Chris bragged about my detective skills at his weekly off-season poker game. I had aided the police with their inquiries before. But I still didn't get what exactly Andie's problem had to do with me, or why she had lost faith in her local police so quickly. "If there's no explanation aside from sabotage, why do you think the police are convinced it was a simple robbery?"

"They're distracted by the value of the seed. It's a big number."

"How big?"

"I paid $35,000 cash for those two buckets."

Whoa. My better judgement screamed at me to shut my mouth, but my curiosity, always the devil on my shoulder, won out. "How do you think I can help?"

"You can investigate. Figure out who hates me that much. Because the seed are so valuable, the police think my robbery was about financial gain for the thief. I'm convinced the motive was to ruin me. Maybe the person who did this thinks it will put me out of business because if I buy more seed, I might not have the cash I need to hire summer staff and run the business. Or maybe they hope the damage will be in the long term. That I won't replace the seed and my crop three years from now will be too small to sustain me." She paused. "Neither is true, by the way. I have the cash to replace the seed. It's not the money I'm worried about so much as the motive."

Chris spoke up for the first time since our little meeting had begun. "I wasn't sure exactly what you could do, Julia, but I figured you could poke around, like you do, and help Andie figure this out."

"This is a different situation." I pushed back, but didn't say more.

"You've learned from what you've done." Chris clearly was heavily invested in having me help his friend.

The three of us looked from one to the other. I sensed there was something more, something Andie wasn't telling me, but whether her reluctance came because she didn't want to talk in front of Chris or for some other reason, I couldn't tell. Once I'd gotten over my surprise that she wasn't a man, my first impression of her was good. She seemed smart and cool and she owned and ran a successful oyster farm.

"Tell you what," I said. "I'll come visit you tomorrow morning and we can talk some more. No commitment. If I don't think I can help, I'll be honest."

"Thank you!" Andie gave me an address on the River Road which I wrote on the blotter. "As for the time, you name it. I'm a farmer, I get up with the sun."

"I'm not a farmer." I worked late into the evening most of the year, either running the Snowden Family Clambake dinner service during tourist season or, with Chris, a restaurant that catered to locals in the off-season. "I'll see you at nine thirty tomorrow morning."

Chris walked Andie out. They clumped down the staircase, both in their heavy boots. The old front door of my mother's house creaked open, good-byes were spoken, and then I heard a single set of footsteps coming back up the stairs.

"You didn't tell me Andie Greatorex is a woman."

Clearly not the greeting Chris had been expecting. He rocked back on his heels. His brow crinkled upward with surprise, emphasizing the lines around his deep green eyes. The lines reflected a lot of laughter, a lot of pain, and a life lived outdoors. "Of course she's a woman."

"How would I know that? On the rare occasions when you do mention her it's always 'Andie this,' 'Andie that.' I pictured a guy." I sounded annoyed because I was.

"Everyone around here knows Andie," he insisted.

That shut me up for a minute. I'd grown up in Busman's Harbor, but I'd been away for boarding school, college, grad school, and work. It was the beginning of my third season back in town running my family's clambake business. People forgot I didn't know everything. "Why did you bring her here? How do you think I can help her?"

Chris looked surprised. "It's what you do, isn't it? Help people who've been involved in crimes."

I'd never quite heard it put that way. "I have, in the past, helped the state police Major Crimes Unit with investigations, but my principle contribution was local knowledge. I don't know anything about Damariscotta. I don't know the cops there. It's a whole other thing."

Chris sat in one of the guest chairs, his long legs sprawled in front of him. "Julia, I wouldn't ask, but Andie's seriously upset. She's a good friend, an old friend, and you like to investigate, at least you appear to. And it's a good time for you to do it."

By 'it's a good time,' he meant it was a quiet time of year business-wise. We had shut down our restaurant, Gus's Too, which we ran as a place for local people to

have a meal or a drink during the off season when everything else was closed. And the Snowden Family Clambake hadn't started up yet. But that didn't mean I wasn't
busy. I looked at the employment applications fanned out
on my desk. I had critical positions to fill at the clambake
before we opened in ten short days. And I had suppliers
to find, including a new primary supplier for our steamers, the soft-shell clams that gave the bake its name. But
Chris was right, my schedule was more flexible now than
it would be at any time until the fall.

"Are all the people in your poker game women?"

Chris laughed and I did, too. "Andie is the only one.
You know Sam for heaven's sake." Sam Rockmaker was
Chris's boss at Crowley's, Busman's Harbor's noisiest,
most touristy bar, where he worked as a bouncer eve-
nings, his third job during the tourist season.

I looked down at the mess on my desk and then up at
Chris, who remained relaxed, casually sprawled in the
chair. "Was there ever anything between you and Andie?"

Even though it made me sound like a jealous nutcase,
it was a reasonable question. Chris of the long, rangy
body, tousled hair, green eyes, and freaking chin dimple,
was as my mother originally described him, "too handsome for his own good." He'd been my middle school
crush when he was a senior, a football captain, and all-
around high school god. No one had been more astonished than me when we'd gotten together after I returned
to town. The interim period had given Chris a decade and
a half as a free-range bachelor. I never quite got used to
being stopped all over town by women asking, "How's
Chris?" or telling me to "Say hi to Chris." That sort of
thing had settled down a good deal over the past year, but

it was still there. Chris, to his credit, was incredibly patient and supportive about my little freak-outs about his past.

"Absolutely not. Andie and I have been friends for ages, but only friends."

I nodded. "I like her. I think we could be friends, too."

CHAPTER TWO

The next morning at 9:32 a.m. my navy-blue Subaru wagon bumped up the long, narrow private road to Great River Oysters. I'd seen the Great River sign out on the River Road hundreds of times as I'd driven from Busman's Harbor to Damariscotta, but I'd never visited the business. At work, I had my hands full of clams and lobsters. I didn't know a thing about oysters.

Andie's company was housed in two connected wooden buildings, painted white. There was a retail outlet for the oysters and barn-like structure that looked like it was used for packing and shipping. A few picnic tables were scattered on a flat piece of lawn, presumably for people who purchased oysters and wanted to eat them on the spot.

A sign on the door to the store said CLOSED, but a red

pickup truck and a beat-up Toyota stood in the dirt parking area. As I approached a kid came out. He looked young and I wondered momentarily why he wasn't in school, but decided he could be a recent high school graduate or a college student already out for the summer.

"Are you Julia? Andie's expecting you. She's down on the dock."

"Thanks." He pointed me to a dirt road that descended steeply toward the river.

There was a strip of woods, about a hundred yards wide on my left as I walked. Through the bright spring leaves, I could see the start of a neighbor's lawn on the other side of it. As I came around a curve at the bottom of the road, a large dock complex with a shed on it came into view.

"Julia!" Andie stood on the end of the dock taking off a wetsuit. "Thanks for coming."

"Happy to. This is quite an operation."

Andie finished removing the suit and hung it to dry. "Let me show you around." She had a bright-red two-piece bathing suit on under the wetsuit. She stepped into a pair of khaki shorts and pulled on a blue cotton shirt as she spoke. The day was bright and sunny, but it was still May in Maine. That morning I'd put my jeans on as usual, but instead of my uniform of flannel-shirt-over-T-shirt, I put on a nice pink top and a navy-blue cardigan. Instead of boots, I'd worn a pair of navy flats I usually reserved for when I was hosting at Gus's Too. Andie looked a little underdressed to me, but she'd just come out of some very cold water.

As we walked down the dock, I was conscious of how Andie towered over me. I'm small but strong from my work at the clambake. Andie, in her looks and movement, radiated power. Whoever had attacked her had a heck of a lot of nerve.

She led me from the main dock to an attached floating platform, opened a white box suspended in the water, stuck in a hand, and pulled out a handful of sand. "These are baby oysters," she said. "A week older than the ones that were stolen."

I bent closer so I could see. "They look like . . ."

"Quinoa." She laughed. "Everybody says that."

"How many oysters is that?" I pointed to her hand.

"This? Maybe five thousand. At this stage, there are sixty thousand of them in each upweller."

"And that's an upweller?"

"These are upwellers." She pointed to the white box, which truly was the size of a breadbox, and five others like it. "They're nurseries for baby oysters," she explained. "The upwellers hang from the dock and a pump system pushes water through to make sure the oysters get plenty of nutrients." She returned the handful to the box. "Well-fed baby oysters grow like crazy. They double in size every day—and they make a lot of poop. Every other day we open each upweller, shift and sort the oysters and rinse away the poop. A lot of the poop will be pushed out by the pumps, but a lot will remain. Some oysters grow faster than others and we move those to another upweller to try to keep similar sizes together."

"And this is what was stolen from you?"

"Yes, the seed intended for those two upwellers." She pointed to two boxes on the end of the row. "We stagger starting the seed in the spring, partly because it's so much work to get them going and partly to spread out the sizes a little."

"What would happen to the seed if it wasn't cared for properly?"

"It would die." She pursed her lips. "And be worthless to anyone."

"Where do you get it?"

"From the hatchery. There's one here on the river, another over on Muscongus Bay. Pretty much every farm on the river uses one or both."

Andie looked across the Damariscotta to rows of black boxes floating on the clear water. "Those are the cages we move them to."

The river was wide at that point. The nearest cages were about fifteen yards from the bank on our side. There were cages floating near the other bank as well. There was plenty of room for boats to pass in between them.

"After three months or so, we move the oysters from the upwellers to the cages," Andie said. "Do you want to see?"

She led me to the boat tied up at the end of the dock, a utilitarian sort of a thing with an inboard motor and plastic crates piled up in the back. I helped with the lines and we motored into the river.

I'd been on a boat on the Damariscotta River many times and always loved it. The day was gorgeous, the sky bright. High white clouds drifted on a field of deep blue. There was something so relaxing and entrancing about the river. I lived and worked on the ocean, which was a beautiful wild thing, but even on a calm day, it had to be approached with caution. The river cradled you in its banks and protected you.

We headed out to strings of floating black cages. Each was about the size and shape of a trombone case. There were groups of them together in many parts of the river, easily visible from where we were. "How many oyster farms are there on the Damariscotta?" I asked.

"Five others, six including Great River. And Midden Bay, but they haven't started harvesting yet. They're new."

"And you all get along?"

Andie steered the boat over to a triple row of cages. "Yes. We work together to keep the environment clean. We talk a lot of business, comparing costs and approaches. The other owners are really the only people in the world who understand my life. Our crews all know each other and party together all summer. By the end of the season they're all great friends." She paused. "At least that's what I've always thought."

"But now you have doubts?"

"The seed is only valuable to someone who has the equipment and knows how to take care of it."

"Can you think of someone in particular?" I asked. "A farmer who resents you or is angry at you for some reason?"

She paused. "These people are my friends. Some of them are really good friends. That's why I prefer to think it was someone who hoped to put me out of business, who didn't care if the oyster seed died."

"Who would want to put you out of business?"

She didn't answer. Instead she used a hook out to pull one of the floating cages toward the boat. She flipped it open and extracted a mesh bag filled with silver-dollar sized oysters. "After the upwellers, we move the oysters to these cages. And then when they're big enough we plant them on the bottom."

"How long will they be in the cages?"

"Three to four months. These guys will be here most of the summer.

"And then you just . . . chuck them?"

She laughed. "Onto the bottom in the area of the river where our lease is, yes."

"But that's tens of thousands of dollars' worth of oysters." I couldn't imagine throwing that kind of money off the side of a boat.

She laughed. "We lose some, but oysters grow where they're planted. They're not like clams. They can't move. A nice piece of hard bottom makes an oyster happy. The bottom in a lot of the river is clay, perfect for oysters."

"And then what happens?"

"A couple of years later, I come along in my wetsuit and scuba gear and pick them up."

"You harvest them all by hand!"

"I do." It clearly made her proud. "When oysters are farmed in tidal bays the water may get shallow enough to harvest them walking on the bottom, wearing waders. But the Damariscotta never gets that shallow. Most of the farms along the river do some dive harvesting but also use draggers. But those are tough on the oysters, tough on other critters, and tough on the bottom. I know exactly what I'm looking for and I only take what I can use. Great River Oysters have a fabulous reputation. Almost all my customers are topflight restaurants. My chefs demand an oyster that looks beautiful and tastes amazing. We have a reputation for delivering exactly that."

She was so proud of her business. I was impressed by her. "Are there oysters right under us now?"

Andie shook her head. "We plant them in a part of our leasehold that's farther out toward the ocean and therefore colder and saltier. It's takes them longer to mature when the water is cold, but they taste even better."

As she steered us back toward the Great River dock, I sat in the boat and watched the banks go by. There were big old houses with enormous lawns and smaller summer cottages built by families of more modest means. There were year-round houses where people who worked on the river and in town lived—lobstermen, oyster farmers, restaurant owners, shopkeepers, and retirees. Wedged in here and there were enormous new houses built in this era when the rich kept getting richer. Every one of them, from mansion to tiny, unwinterized cottage, would have the same beautiful view and access to the river.

From our vantage point in the boat I spotted something on the bank I hadn't noticed on land. A compact, two-story bungalow with a deep screened-in porch in the woods between the Great River buildings and the big house next door.

"Who lives there?" I pointed.

"I do. The store, shipping barn, and my cottage were originally outbuildings for that big house beyond the tree line." I followed her finger to a shingle-style summer house with a wide lawn and a modest dock on the river. Its weathered shingles were dark gray, its trim painted dark brown. It had the turrets and bay windows typical of its style. It was enormous, a three-story creepy castle dominating the landscape.

"Living on the farm property makes my life simpler,"

Andie said. "Also, I love my house. It has the same view I look at all day, but on a summer evening, put me on that porch with a beer, listening to Roseanne Cash, watching the eagles and seals. Nothing is better."

Nothing is better. I felt the same way about Morrow Island where we ran our clambakes.

Andie had cut the motor and we drifted on the river. The Damariscotta is tidal. There's always a strong current, but Andie seemed in command. "How's Chris doing?" she asked.

The change of subject surprised me. "Fine, I think."

"That's good to hear," Andie responded. "Because that whole thing with his brother was . . . intense. And I'm sure it brings up all the stuff he's had to deal with related to his mom and her Huntington's disease."

"You know about that?" I was stunned. Chris had only told me the previous spring that his mother had Huntington's, and there was a fifty-fifty chance he had it too. And that was after we'd been living together for two years.

"Yeah, I know about it," Andie said. "Chris and I go way back."

Another piece of distracting information.

We floated a little longer, each of us lost in our thoughts. Then I took advantage of the quiet to ask her the question that had nagged at me since the day before. "Andie, I can tell you have a theory about why this robbery happened. If you want me to help you, you have to tell me what it is."

Wordlessly, Andie guided the boat to a wooden float in the middle of the river and tied us up to it. There were lobster buoys in the water along with oyster cages belonging to multiple farms, but it was early in the season and we had the place to ourselves.

"You know more than you're telling me," I insisted. "You have an idea about who robbed you even if you don't have facts. I can't help if you're not straight with me."

"I'm sorry," she said. "I hate thinking about this. I hate thinking that someone I know wants to hurt my business."

"But you do have an idea why." I pressed her.

"I've applied to quadruple my lease holdings on the river. It will take me from being a small, boutique operation to be the largest in the area. Some people don't like it."

Now we were getting somewhere. "What people, specifically?"

"Lots of people. For example, some of the other oyster farmers are nervous about the application."

"Why?"

"They're worried that after granting my lease the state will think there's too much area on the river used for aquaculture and the other farmers won't be allowed to expand."

"Is there anyone who's particularly anxious," I asked, "or who has threatened you?"

"No. I swear."

"Anyone else?"

"The lobstermen aren't happy with more of the river going to aquaculture," she answered. "They think we're horning in on their bottom."

"I know lobstermen work the river, but lobsters live in saltwater, and river water is fresh."

"The river is fresh at its source, Damariscotta Lake, but because it's tidal it gets saltier as it gets closer to the sea. This part of the river is brackish, a mix perfect for oysters, but lobsters can live here, too."

"Is there a lobsterman who is particularly upset about your plan to expand, or one you're afraid of?"

She shook her head, but I didn't believe her. She definitely felt threatened by someone, but I couldn't tell if she was lying to me or to herself.

"Who else?" I asked.

"Some of the homeowners along the river don't want any more leases. The truth is they'd like us gone completely, but they know the oyster farms have been too successful to get rid of. They see my lease application as something of a last stand."

"Why do the homeowners object?" I didn't get it. The oyster farms were quiet neighbors. They provided jobs and attracted tourists who filled the businesses downtown.

"It's some of the summer people with the big houses. They don't like the way the cages look. They claim the oyster poop pollutes the river when really oysters are filter feeders who clean the water. And they say our cages, floats, and whatnots get in the way of their fancy sailboats."

"Sounds ridiculous."

"It is." Andie shuddered. "I don't want to think it was any of these people. But there's a hearing on my lease application two days from now, and I believe the robbery of my oyster seed was a warning."

"You think the robbery was meant to intimidate you into withdrawing the lease application, not to put you out of business," I confirmed. "That's slightly different."

"I don't know," she said. "Some people, a tiny minority, won't be happy until we're all gone."

I nodded, taking it all in. "Tell me exactly what happened when you were robbed."

"Monday morning I drove back from picking up the spat at the hatchery."

"Which hatchery?"

"Crane's Oystery, right here in town."

I nodded. "Go on."

"I drove my truck all the way down to the dock. The buckets are heavy. I didn't want to carry them down the hill." She hesitated.

"Did you sense anyone following you?"

"Absolutely not." Her ponytail whipped from side to side as she shook her head.

"And then what?"

"I got out of the truck, opened the back and pulled out the buckets. That's when it happened. A man dashed out of the woods and grabbed both buckets. I shouted and got a hold of his sweatshirt. He turned and kicked me in the stomach. I went down on the ground, hard. He ran back into the woods and disappeared. It was over in a matter of seconds."

We both turned and looked at the strip of woods. Dense with trees and new spring undergrowth, it extended from the riverbank up the hill and out of sight, the green broken only by Andie's cottage.

"Describe the man."

"He was dressed in black, black jeans, black hoodie. He wore a black ski mask."

"Tall or short, slim or heavy, young or old?"

"Tall, lean, but strong. I didn't see his face, but from the way he moved I think he was young."

"Did you recognize him? I mean despite the mask, did he seem the slightest bit familiar?"

"No!"

Her response raised several questions, but I stayed on the main path. "Which way did he run?"

Andie stood up in the boat and pointed toward the shore. "I parked my truck at the bottom of the road next to the dock. I was at the back of it when he assaulted me. He ran off through the woods toward my house."

"Is there access to the road directly from your house? Could he have had a vehicle parked there?"

"No. To get to my cottage you come up the farm road. There's a turnoff to the house right before you come to the shop. He could have stayed in the trees all the way to the River Road," Andie said. "I assume he had a vehicle parked there. But he could also have run across my neighbor's lawn. I was on the ground. I couldn't see far."

"Did you see a strange vehicle parked on the River Road when you turned into the farm road?"

"Not that I remember, but I'm not sure that's something I would have taken note of."

"Do you have security cameras around the farm?"

"There's nothing of value. Some knickknacks in the shop and whatever cash is in the till. The oysters are the only thing worth money and we ship them out the day they're harvested. I've never seen any reason for a lot of security."

"The upwellers are worth money," I pointed out. "Or what's in them is."

"I know." Andie sighed. "It didn't occur to me that anyone would steal them."

"Okay. What did you do after the guy ran?"

"I got up, dusted myself off, and then went as fast as I could go to the truck to get my phone which was in the console by the driver's seat. I called 911. When the dispatcher heard I'd been attacked she kept me on the line until the officers arrived."

"How long did that take?"

"Maybe seven to ten minutes. Two separate patrol cars came, one cop in each. They took all the information and searched the woods and the road, but the guy was long gone. They asked if I wanted to go to the hospital, but by then I could tell I wasn't hurt badly."

"What did the police say they were going to do?"

"They informed the local oyster farms to report anyone who came along offering them cheap seed. They took photos of the extra buckets I have in the shed and asked their officers to be on the lookout for ones that looked like mine. They said they'd check around to see if anyone had heard anything." Andie shrugged. "Nothing so far on any of those fronts. At least not that they've told me about."

I considered where to take the conversation next. "Who knew you were picking up the seed on that day, at that time?"

Andie crossed her tan arms and thought. "People at the hatchery, I suppose. When you place your order, you tell them the date and time you'll show up, so the order is ready."

"It could have been someone from the hatchery who robbed you."

"I suppose. They'd be one of the few places that could take care of the seed and therefore realize the value. But even if it was a rogue employee, if they did it to more than one customer it wouldn't take long to figure out what was happening."

"Either you're the beginning of a crime wave—"

"Or I was specifically targeted," Andie finished. "I think that's more likely it."

"What about your employees. Did they know you'd gone to pick up the seed?"

Andie frowned. It wasn't pleasant to think about people you knew and trusted doing something like this. "I have a really small crew right now. I'm in the process of staffing up for the summer."

"Me, too." The lack of summer employees had been a problem in coastal Maine for years, especially recently with the crackdown on visas for foreign workers.

"It's just three employees. Josh runs the store," Andie said.

"I met him on the way in."

"And Karin and Althea do the sorting, packing and shipping. Neither were on the property at the time. I can't believe it's any of them. None of them are tall, lean men, in any event."

"But they have friends," I pointed out. "One of them might have inadvertently mentioned you were picking up something relatively small and portable worth thirty-five thousand dollars. Did the police talk to your employees?"

Andie nodded. "They were interviewed. Freaked them out a little, poor things."

I finally asked about the thing that had been bothering me. "If you didn't recognize your attacker, why are you convinced it was someone from the specific circle of people who would be upset by the expansion of your business? Don't you know virtually all of them by sight?"

Andie was quiet for a long time. "I think whoever attacked me was hired by someone else. I don't know my attacker, I'm sure."

Hired to commit a felony. That sounded super-serious. But aside from her fears and assumptions, Andie was giving me little to work with. I tried again.

"If you can't think of who might have hired someone to rob you, was there anything that made you uneasy before the assault? Was there any build up to it?"

"Like what?" Andie frowned like her brain was working hard, honestly trying to come up with some nugget of information for me.

I tried to think of examples. This was new territory for me, too. "Like graffiti on your sign down on the road, vandalism to your mailbox, nails in your driveway. Has your truck been keyed?" I stopped, my imagination failing me.

Andie's forehead was still pinched together over her nose. "Nothing," she assured me, followed by a slight hesitation. "Aside from the usual."

That stopped me cold. "What's the usual?"

"People interfering with our gear, cutting loose the buoys that mark the boundaries of our leases, turning over cages."

"That's usual?" It didn't sound usual to me.

"It's petty harassment. It happens to all the oyster farmers, not just me."

"Who does it and why?"

She spread out her strong arms and rolled her neck,

working out a kink. "We assume it's the lobstermen having their fun, or maybe pleasure boaters. Everyone complains about it, but nobody does anything." She looked directly at me. Her hazel eyes were flecked with green. "I don't think these little things have anything to do with what happened to me. Whoever messes with our gear, there's no harm done. They don't steal oysters or dump the cages which would really cost us. They're just letting us know they're out there."

I considered what she'd said. "Has this petty harassment as you call it increased lately? Have you been targeted more than others?"

"It has increased, but it's May. The traffic on the river is increasing. Lobstermen are dropping more traps. Pleasure boats are being put back in the water. Really, Julia, this stuff is like background noise in my life. Something I live with."

And that was that. "You can't think of anyone else who would be out to destroy your business or stop your lease expansion?" I was frustrated with her. Could she really not think of a single specific person who wanted to hurt her, or was she unable to face that someone she knew, maybe someone she counted as a friend, wanted to put her out of business?

Andie didn't answer. Wordlessly, she untied the boat from the float, started the engine and headed us back to shore.

After we tied up, Andie took me to the sorting shed on the dock where her summer crew would size the oysters. "They'll be here later to sort the ones I harvested this morning." She explained that the biggest ones with the best shell color and shape, the "select," would be shipped to fancy restaurants all over the United States. The merely "choice" would be headed to lesser places. In the corner, there were a half dozen white plastic buckets with metal handles, the kind you get at the hardware store for doing household chores. GREAT RIVER OYSTERS had been stenciled on each of them in bold, black letters.

"Are those buckets like the ones that were taken?"

Andie nodded. I took my phone out of my jeans pocket and snapped a photo. She led me out of the shed and we climbed the steep hill back to the retail store and shipping barn.

The barn was empty. Andie explained there were no shipments going out that day. "By a month from now we'll be loading six trucks a day."

"I thought people didn't eat oysters in a month without an R in it." I was half-joking. I knew people ate oysters year-round, but I'd often heard the saying.

"That's a myth. Oysters spawn in the summer and some people think they become less tasty during that period, but other people prefer them. The hatcheries breed a new kind of oyster that doesn't spawn and some of the farms buy those. Also, in warmer climates summer can bring algae blooms that contaminate the oysters, but the water here stays so cold that's not an issue."

"The seed you bought, was it the kind that doesn't spawn?"

"No," Andie said. "I'm a purist when it comes to oysters, but I don't judge others that use them."

I couldn't see how the type of seed would have to do with her robbery one way or the other. Andie led me through the mostly empty barn through a side door into the retail store.

The kid I'd met on the way in was emptying boxes filled with metal mesh gloves onto a shelf. He had a long torso and stubby legs that added up to him being quite short. Long, dark bangs covered his eyebrows and barely missed his eyes. Certainly not Andie's tall attacker.

"Hi Josh. This is Julia."

"Hi." He flicked his bangs out of his eyes with a quick shake of his head. "We met earlier."

The shop was open and airy and, in addition to oysters, sold all manner of oyster-related gizmos, shucking knives and gloves, and oyster plates along with T-shirts, baseball hats, aprons and other items with the Great River Oysters name and logo. "We're stocking up for tourist season," Andie explained to me.

"Great space," I said. Andie went to a glass-fronted refrigerator. "Soft drink?" she asked.

"Thanks."

The sound of a car door slamming came from the driveway. I glanced out to see a small young woman running across the lawn. She didn't look happy.

The door to the store flew open and banged against the inside wall. A bell over the door clanged in protest. "I caught you!" the young woman shouted at Andie. "Now you have to pay me."

Andie closed the refrigerator door and looked up. Her calm, deliberate motions seemed to inflame the woman further.

"I texted you and texted you. You owe me my check!" She ran at Andie. Josh watched the scene, rooted to his spot but clearly torn. His instincts probably told him he should defend his boss. On the other hand, Andie had a least six inches and thirty pounds on him and probably could defend herself.

In the end, no physical defense was needed. "Your check is here." Andie spoke as if the check had been requested in a reasonable way. "I texted you I'd have it ready."

Andie went behind the cashier's stand and plucked a key chain from a bowl on the counter. She inserted one of the keys, opened a drawer and pulled out a white, number ten envelope. There was handwriting on the front, but I couldn't read it from where I stood.

The young woman snatched the envelope, opened it, looked at the check, whirled around and stalked out, slamming the door as she did.

"Lovely." Andie crossed the room back to the refrigerator and asked, "Blueberry soda or root beer?"

I opted for the root beer and followed her outside. We settled at one of the picnic tables. "She seemed upset," I observed mildly. Why hadn't Andie told me about her?

"Ex-employee," Andie said. "I hired her to help in the store. We'll expand our open hours starting Memorial Day. She was here all of two days, and then no-showed. She left so little impression I practically forgot about her."

"Except for the texts demanding her two days' pay," I said.

"Except for those," Andie admitted.

"Did you fire her before you got robbed?"

Andie had to think about it. "Yes."

"Did you mention a recently fired, disgruntled employee to the police?"

"I didn't know she was disgruntled. She showed up for the first two days she was on the schedule and then disappeared. Ghosted me completely. Didn't respond to phone messages or texts with an explanation. I had to fire her by text. She still didn't respond. At the time I talked to the police, I assumed she'd abandoned her job because she found something better. It happens, especially at the beginning of the season."

"I'm aware." Keeping the Snowden Family Clambake staffed with good people was a huge challenge. I especially hated firing people, but sometimes things didn't work out. "Then what happened?"

"Yesterday, I got like half a dozen texts from her demanding to be paid for the two days' work. I made up the check, put it in the drawer and texted her to come and get it."

"What's her name?"

"Lacey. Lacey Brenneman. I wouldn't even have remembered it except that I just cut the check."

"You need to tell the police about her. 'Disgruntled employee,' is a classic. You shouldn't withhold information from the cops. It won't help your case."

"Okay." Andie was reluctant, but she agreed.

I sipped the cool root beer. It tasted great, sweet and spicy. I needed the liquid after following Andie around the farm all morning in the sun. "How did you get into the business?" I asked.

"I was a marine biology major at UMaine, Orono. Historically, the Damariscotta River had a thriving oyster population. There are huge middens, piles of oyster shells consumed by native people more than two thousand years ago, along its banks. But then, in the nineteenth century, the river got polluted. Its lower end, where we are now, died completely, couldn't sustain life.

"It took a long time, but by the 1980s the river had come back, and some of the people who later became my professors at UMaine realized the environment of the Damariscotta was perfect for oysters. It's cold and brackish, and rich with plankton. There's a formation near where we stopped today, Glidden Ledge that keeps the water on the town side pretty warm, at least for Maine, and the water beyond it is ocean-cold. The warmer water is perfect for growing the babies, the upwellers and the cages, and the cold water is perfect for planting and letting the oysters finish their growth. So they founded the first farms here. At the time it was a daring experiment.

"The farms were established by the time I went to school. I was fascinated. I did internship for two summers and then worked at Glidden Point Oyster Farm for four years doing every job they would let me. I particularly loved caring for the upwellers and diving for the harvest. Then I raised my stake, got my first lease and started Great River." She paused and sipped her blueberry soda.

"It must take capital to start an oyster farm, not to have a crop for three years. And the riverfront property must have been expensive. How did you raise it?" I knew all about undercapitalized small businesses. A silent partner had to rescue the Snowden Family Clambake three years earlier.

Andie didn't hesitate. "I started with a partner, Mack Owen. He's a friend of Chris's, used to play poker with us. Do you know him?"

"I don't know him through Chris, but I've heard of him. He's Mack's Oyster Shack, right?" Mack's was a popular eatery in Damariscotta, located on the riverfront downtown. A great place to eat out in the summer, or so I'd been told. I worked at the Snowden Family Clambake fourteen hours a day, seven days a week during the tourist season, so I'd never been to the restaurant. But I'd sent a lot of our customers there who asked where they should have their next meal. Everyone who'd gotten back to me had raved about the place.

"That's right," Andie said. "Mack and I started off as partners in the farm. Then we started the restaurant. We wanted a place where visitors could see how great our oysters were. Also, since we sell to restaurants, we wanted to be able to talk knowledgeably with our chef customers."

I was confused. "Are you still business partners?"

"No. As time went on, he became more interested in the restaurant and I became more interested in the farm. We agreed to buy each other out and each focus on one business."

"That must have been a complicated transaction."

"It was. It wasn't a straight-up trade. The farm was worth a lot more than the restaurant at that point, so I had to come up with the money to compensate Mack for the extra value. My mom died around that time and I used the money she left me to buy Mack out. It was worth it, believe me. In the beginning it was great to have a partner to bounce things off of, but by the time we split up the business I wasn't interested in sharing decision-making about the farm. Mack felt the same way about the restaurant. That's when I bought the cottage, too."

"How long ago was this?"

"Five years ago this fall."

"Was it amicable?" Andie was looking for someone who wanted to sabotage her business. An ex-partner might be emotionally invested enough to hate.

Andie smiled. "There were moments . . . But we got through it successfully and we're still friends."

"So Mack wouldn't have any reason to . . . ?"

"Good heavens, no!"

We finished the sodas. "I'll poke around today and see what I can find out," I told her. "No guarantees."

"No guarantees," she agreed.

"In the meantime, be careful. Lock your doors. Be aware of what's going on around you."

"I'll do my best." Andie looked around at the peaceful farm, the shop, the picnic tables, the woods. "I'm outdoors a lot and at this time of year I'm usually alone."

We stood up from the picnic table and hugged, newfound friends. Then she walked me to my car.

CHAPTER THREE

It was eleven o'clock by the time my Subaru was back on the River Road. I called Chris. "What are you doing?" I asked when he picked up.

"Opening summer houses," he said in a what-else-would-I-be-doing tone of voice. A part of Chris's landscaping business was caring for summer homes, and that included a spring clean-up of the yard and general shakedown of the house—turning on the water or the heat if needed, checking for varmints and storm damage. He had a ton of houses to open before their owners arrived for Memorial Day.

"Do you want to meet me for lunch? I just got done meeting with Andie."

"Sounds intriguing." Ordinarily, I wouldn't have interrupted Chris's work to pursue some interest of my own, but he had gotten me into this. "Where?" he asked.

"Mack's Oyster Shack. I'd like to get there before the lunch crowd so we can have a conversation with Mack."

"I can be there in half an hour."

I drove from Great River Oysters to downtown Damariscotta and found a parking space on Main Street, something that would never happen once the season began. I wandered in and out of the shops to kill the time—Sheepscot River Pottery, Sherman's Maine Coast Book Shop, and not one but two locations of Reny's, Maine's beloved discount department store, where I ended up spending some money. It was a kind of hard-core touristing I rarely got to do, and by the time I walked, carrying my shopping bag, back toward Mack's location by the bridge coming into town, Chris's pickup was in the restaurant's parking lot.

He was in the cab, squinting at his phone, when I knocked on his window. He jumped and then saw me and laughed. "You scared me." He got out of the truck.

"I can tell."

He looked around the nearly empty lot. "I didn't see your car."

"I parked on the street."

Mack's Oyster Shack was a low slung, rustic, brown-shingled building on a point surrounded on two sides by the river. A banner hung from the eaves. In blue letters on a white background it read SUMMER OPENING along with a date, the Friday of the long Memorial Day weekend.

"What am I doing here?" Chris asked.

"I want to see if Mack has any ideas about who might sabotage Andie. I hear you're old friends, so I thought you might smooth the way."

"I suppose I deserve this." Chris stuffed his hands in his jeans' pockets. "What did Andie tell you?"

I gave him a quick summary of the crime, the assailant, and the police response. By the time I was done, two more cars had pulled into the parking lot. "Let's go in," Chris said.

"Before we go in, tell me about Andie and Mack. And you and Andie and Mack for that matter."

"Ah." Chris shifted his weight in his boots. "Not much to tell. I met Andie the summer we both got out of high school. She's from somewhere near Portland. We worked together in the kitchen at the Seaward Inn. I was a prep chef and she waited tables. A whole gang of us hung out together."

Chris's story that he and Andie had never been an item was getting less and less credible. "And then?"

"And then she went off to college at Orono and I got a job at the lumber yard for the winter. I didn't expect to see her again." Chris hadn't gone to college, despite a full scholarship to the University of New Hampshire. He'd stayed home to care for his younger sister while she finished high school. "But the next summer most of us got together and we hung out when we weren't working. Those friendships are the core of the poker group now."

"Even Sam Rockmaker?"

"Even Sam. He didn't always own Crowley's. He was young and crazy like the rest of us."

"Was Mack Owen a part of that gang from the Seaward Inn?"

"No. He came later, when Andie brought him around."

"When was that?"

"When they started going out. They worked together

at Glidden Point, so I guess after Andie graduated from college, but not long after."

"Wait a minute. Andie and Mack were a couple-couple, not just business partners?" Strange that Andie hadn't mentioned that. She said she wanted my help, but I wasn't so sure.

"Yeah, for like ten years. They founded and ran the farm as a couple."

"Were they married?"

"No. But it was like they were married. We all treated them like they were married."

"Then what happened?"

"One night they showed up for poker and calm as anything told us they were splitting up. Mack was taking the restaurant, Andie the farm. Honestly, it took me pretty far into the conversation to understand they were also splitting up as a couple."

"No anger, no upset, no tears?"

"Not that I ever saw. From either of them."

It was long enough ago it was hard to imagine that even if there had been hard feelings at the time there might still the kind of anger burning that would result in the attempt to destroy someone's business. "Do they still both play in the game?"

"Andie does. Mack has dropped out."

"Was it too uncomfortable?"

Chris shrugged his shoulders, well-muscled from his work in his landscaping business. "No. Not at all. He played for a while after they broke up, but then he got married, had kids. Too busy. You know how it is."

Clearly Mack had moved on. The idea that he might be behind the attack on Andie seemed unlikely.

"Why do you think they split up?" I asked.

"They said they'd grown apart. But who knows, really? Nobody understands anybody else's relationship. Let's get lunch."

As we'd talked, another car had pulled into the parking lot. The window to talk to Mack before lunch got busy was probably rapidly closing. "Sure. Let's eat," I said.

The entrance to the restaurant was low-ceilinged and dark, but then the room opened up to walls of windows and views of the river. The structure was on the smallish side for a restaurant, but tables on the decks at the front and side of the building would triple the seating in the summer. The inside space was dominated by two bars. At the back of the room was a half-moon shaped oyster bar—a countertop surrounded by a vast bed of ice in which the raw oysters were displayed. On the other side, in the center of the room was a square bar with taps and liquor bottles and wine glasses hanging from racks above it.

A young hostess approached to seat us but was interrupted when the man behind the oyster bar yelled, "Chris! Over here!"

"Thanks." Chris gestured to the hostess that we'd seat ourselves.

The man behind the oyster bar came out to greet us. He was average height and narrow-shouldered, sinewy. A hank of dark brown hair fell across his forehead, dangling over his large brown eyes. "Chris. It's been way too long since you've been here, man. Do you ever leave Busman's Harbor?" He and Chris embraced.

"Mack Owen, I'd like you to meet Julia Snowden." Chris stepped aside and I put out my hand.

"So you're Chris's Julia. At last. We're not going to shake. We're going to hug."

I smiled and returned the hug. I wasn't used to being "Chris's Julia." In our world, I was very much my own me, but Mack was Chris's friend, so I understood.

"Come, come. Eat, eat," Mack urged us. We sat on tall stools and he returned to behind the bar.

I examined the oysters displayed on the ice. They were noticeably different sizes, some the size of my palm, others smaller. Some of the shells were deeper and rounder, others flatter, some mostly had brown striations, others were entirely blue and gray. The name of the farm they had come from was displayed on a small sign above each section. Andie's Great River oysters were the most uniform in size, shape, and color.

"It's terrific to see you," Mack said to Chris. "Can I get you a beer?"

"Sure," Chris said. "How are Ming and the girls?"

"Fine, fine. I don't see enough of them this time of year, you know. We're getting ready for our summer opening. I'm trying to hire enough help."

"Tell me about it," I said. Andie was looking for staff. I was looking for staff. Mack was looking for staff. If we were lucky enough to find them, they would have to be trained.

"You get it. Beer or wine?" Mack asked me.

"Iced tea, please."

Mack called across the mostly empty restaurant to the bartender inside the square bar. "Sam Adams and an iced tea over here, please."

"Coming!" the cheerful young woman called back.

"We saw the banner out front," Chris said.

"In the winter we're mostly a locals place," Mack told

us. "Only this room is open. Now the snowbirds are fil
tering back from the south, and a lot of the summer people open their houses and put their boats in the water over
Memorial Day weekend. It's crazy."

"Tell me about it," Chris repeated the line and we
laughed.

"We had a 'locals' night' last Friday to say good-bye to
the peace and quiet. We'll have the 'summer opening' a
week from Friday for the long Memorial Day weekend."
Mack waved a hand across the bed of ice. "Can I choose
for you?"

"Yes, please." Chris nodded enthusiastically.

"Are they different breeds?" I asked.

"All oysters in the whole east coast of the United
States are the same breed," Mack said. "They're different
because of where they're grown. Oysters are filter-feeders,
their taste reflects the water they grow in." He was
frowning slightly, moving up and down the bar picking
different oysters from the rows. "Are you familiar with
the wine term 'terroir?'"

I hadn't grown up in the food service business for
nothing. "It means wine takes on the taste of the environment in the place where the grapes are grown," I said.
"The wine is distinct because only grapes grown in the
soil, topography, and climate in that specific vineyard
could produce it."

"Exactly," Mack said. "With oysters we talk about
'merroir.' The oyster gets its flavor from the nutrients,
bottom, current and temperature of the specific river or
bay it grows in. You're going to try a variety, so you can
see."

"These oysters come from all different places?" I
asked.

"They all come from right here in the Damariscotta River," Mack assured me. "I wouldn't have it any other way."

"And yet they're different," I said.

"You tell me when you eat them, but yes. All the farms grow different tasting oysters."

"Could you identify oysters from each farm blind-folded?"

Mack laughed. "I can and I have." He shucked the oysters he'd selected for us. Wearing a heavy mesh glove on the hand that held the oyster, he placed it on a towel on the countertop and shoved a small knife into the hinge of the shell. He turned the knife and wiggled it until the hinge popped loose. Explaining his movements as he worked, Mack ran the knife along the flat side of the oyster to cut the muscle that attached it to the shell and took the top off. Then he cut the bottom muscle and set the round side of the shell and the oyster on a round tray of ice and moved on to the next one.

"That must be sharp." I cast a leery eye on the knife.

"Not at all." Mack handed me a clean knife from a container on the counter. Like the one he held, it had a distinctive, thick blue plastic handle that matched the colors of the napkins and seat cushions in the restaurant. The words MACK'S OYSTER SHACK, DAMARISCOTTA, MAINE were printed on it in white letters along with an oyster shell logo. "Run your finger along the sides," he instructed. "Watch out for the point, though. It's super sharp."

The knife was thick and the sides, as Mack said, were smooth and rounded. I put a tentative finger on the point and pulled it away quickly. Super sharp, indeed.

He shucked a dozen oysters so fast I could barely follow the swift movement of his hands. As he worked, he placed each oyster in its bottom shell on the platter of ice. When he was done, he added enamel tags with the names of an oyster farm on each, lemon wedges, and a stainless-steel cup of clear sauce and offered the platter to us with a flourish.

"These are the Norembagas, Glidden Points, Dodge Coves, Mook Seas, Pemaquids, and Great Rivers." He pointed to where each of the oysters were on the platter, a pair from six different farms.

Chris picked up a Great River and examined it. "Beautiful," he said. "The plump oyster, deep cup, the shell." I wasn't surprised Chris knew about oysters. He was a chef and devoted foodie with an abiding curiosity about anything edible. He slurped it down in one go. "Fantastic."

"Agreed," Mack said. "Andie's are the best."

They both looked expectantly at me. "Now you," Mack said.

"Umm."

His brow creased. "You've eaten oysters before, right?"

"Yes, but cooked. My aunt makes the most amazing oyster stuffing."

Chris was astonished. "You're kidding. I've seen you eat cherrystones and sushi. You love seafood."

"Yes."

"Don't worry," Mack said. "We get lots of first timers in here. Take it like this." He picked up the shell and showed me. "Eat it from the wide end. Don't swallow it whole. Chew once or twice to get all the flavors." He poured a tiny bit of the sauce on it. "This is a mignonette, a simple sauce of vinegar, shallots and pepper that's meant to balance the briny, creaminess of the oyster. Now go."

"Umm."

"You are going to love this." Chris had no doubt.

So I did it. Call me adventurous, call it peer pressure. Whatever. I did exactly as instructed. The briny, fresh flavor of the oyster with a flash of sweetness at the finish flooded my mouth and flew across my tongue. It was delicious.

Chris watched my reaction. "You liked it. I told you so. Want to try another one? It only gets more enjoyable."

As Chris and I ate the remaining oysters, Mack told us about how each farm cultivated its crop. Some grew the oysters entirely in cages, most planted them on the bottom, some for two years, some for three. The oysters from each farm were distinctive—brinier, sweeter, meatier, creamier, slightly metallic at the finish.

"Oysters are really having a moment, aren't they?" I said to Mack as we ate.

"They are," Mack agreed. "Oysters go in and out of fashion. They were huge in the late 1800s, a major source of protein. In the 1890s New Yorkers ate an average of six hundred oysters a year."

"What happened?" I asked.

"The rivers around the big cities got too polluted. Shipping shellfish wasn't practical. Oysters fell out of favor. This latest passion for them started with the sushi craze. Sushi got Americans used to eating raw fish again and oysters have blown up from there." Mack gestured toward the tables, which were filling up. "We have a full menu in the restaurant. Oyster stew, oysters Rockefeller, but also fish, lobster, even steaks. But the draw to the restaurant is our raw oysters. We sell more every year. Excuse me." Mack went off to help another couple at the bar select their oysters.

When Mack returned, Chris steered the conversation

around to my reason for being there. "Did you hear what happened to Andie?" he asked, casually, like an interested friend. The weekly area paper, with its closely read police column, wouldn't be out until the next day. But if Mack's place was a hangout for locals in the off season, he would know. He probably interacted with someone from each the oyster farms every day while buying their product. He'd have heard.

"Yup. Her seed got stolen. Shame." His brow creased in a scowl. "Big hit for her."

"Any rumors around town, about who it might have been?"

"Nothing official. Lots of rumors. You know how small towns are. Gossip is the main hobby of everyone who comes in here."

"What are the rumors?" I asked.

"Usual suspects I would say. Lobstermen. They feel embattled, like the aquaculture is encroaching on their territory."

"Is there anyone who had a particular beef with Andie? She believes it was a specific, targeted crime," Chris said.

"Does she now? Bob Campbell's the leader of that lot around here. If anyone knows, he would."

Chris raised an eyebrow at me. I didn't acknowledge it. "How often do you see Andie?" Chris asked Mack.

"Not often," Mack said. "I see her delivery driver a lot more than I see her. Is she still playing in the poker game?"

Chris said she was.

"Then you see her more than I do."

We finished our oysters. Chris and Mack had the expected argument about the bill. Mack insisted it was on the house and Chris eventually gave in. Mack came around from behind the oyster bar and hugged each of us. "Don't let it be so long 'til the next time," he said. "Bring your fine lady around again soon."

When we got out to the parking lot, I asked Chris, "What did you think?"

"The oysters were delicious."

"About Mack."

"Mack wouldn't hurt Andie. Physically, financially, in any way at all. Did Andie say it was him?"

"No. Andie said specifically it wasn't him."

"See."

"She also said it wasn't her angry ex-employee, or one of the summer people who hates the oyster farm, or any of the other farmers. Andie believes whoever did it, or whoever hired the person who did it, was out to hurt her business, but she's having trouble getting her head around the idea that someone she knows would do that to her."

We had reached his truck. "I get it," he said. "I've got to get back to work. What will you do?"

"Go to see my uncle. Bob Campbell."

CHAPTER FOUR

Ten minutes later, I drove down the long driveway at my Aunt Sharon and Uncle Bob Campbell's house. I hadn't been in the least surprised when Mack gave my uncle's name as the leader of the lobstermen who hauled on the river. I already knew it. Aunt Sharon and Uncle Bob were the reason I'd spent time in Damariscotta, the reason I'd spent hours on a boat on the river even before Andie took me out. Uncle Bob was a genial man. He was also ambitious and willing to put in the work to back it up. He was a successful, full-time lobsterman, who didn't need a winter job to keep his business afloat. The kind the others called a highliner. Success commanded respect.

My aunt and uncle's Cape Cod-style house was on the other side of the river and a little more toward town than Andie's place. Their property had been clearly visible from Great River Farm. I tried to remember the last time I'd seen them. It had been long. Too long.

Aunt Sharon was my father's sister, the next oldest, after him, in a family of four siblings. I had spent my childhood enmeshed in my dad's big, boisterous family, with grandparents, aunts, uncles, and cousins. Every Patriot's Day, a holiday unique to Maine and Massachusetts, we had a barbecue at my parents' house whether the April temperatures cooperated or not. Even when there was snow on the ground, that party was the official opening of the spring season, the busy but peaceful time when we prepared for the arrival of the summer people and tourists.

I had spent the first twenty-five Thanksgivings of my life in the white, antique Cape Cod house with the green shutters and the Damariscotta River flowing behind it. There'd been touch football games on the lawn, football on TV, the rise and fall of chatter and laughter all day. And finally the meal. Everyone brought something, but Aunt Sharon supplied the turkey and the luscious oyster dressing. In the car, on a sunny day in May, my mouth watered thinking about it.

When my dad died the gatherings had ended. Honestly the first couple of years after he was gone, I think they couldn't bear to see us. We couldn't bear to see them, and Dad's siblings couldn't bear to see one another. The hole in the family was too big, too visible. After that initial jolt, the family got complicated as families do. Both my grandparents were long dead by then. My cousins were marrying and having children. Many of them lived out of state. I had, too, until three years earlier. Now we only saw each other at weddings and funerals, and not even all of those. I had heard Aunt Sharon and Uncle Bob spent Thanksgivings with my cousin Francie and her young family in New Jersey.

While I sat in my car, memories swirling, the dark green door of the house opened, and Aunt Sharon was on the doorstep. "Julia Snowden! Come in."

Aunt Sharon was a large woman. She'd always been heavy and had added pounds with the years. I climbed the steps and she moved forward and hugged me to her ample bosom. "I am happy to see you, dear." I was so comfortable in her arms; tears sprang to my eyes. I'd been back in the area all this time. Why hadn't I visited sooner?

"I just put a pot on," she said. I had never not known her to have just put a pot of coffee on.

I followed her into the house, wiping the spring mud off my nice flats before I entered and then leaving them by the front door. Everything was exactly as I remembered, though the house was even tinier. How did we all fit on those long-ago Thanksgiving Days? The wallpapered living room had the same Winslow Homer prints on the walls. The kitchen had the same fake stone Formica countertops. The big, white refrigerator hummed away against the far wall. The electric coffee pot percolated, glub, glub, glub. It was *The Land Time Forgot.* Even my mother, who resisted change with all her will, had a fancy new-fangled coffee machine she'd finally learned to use.

Through the window I glimpsed Uncle Bob as he tied his lobster boat, *My Sharona*, up to his dock. That he could have his mooring at his house was unusual. Most lobstermen had to walk or drive to a nearby marina or harbor where they kept their boats, but Uncle Bob and Aunt's Sharon's house, with its long river frontage, provided convenient dockage. My uncle left most of his gear on his boat, but he lugged a few items to the shed in his backyard and stowed them. From the distance I couldn't make out what they were.

Uncle Bob trudged across the lawn and disappeared down the bulkhead, as New Englanders called the entrance to the cellar when it consisted of steps covered by an angled door. I knew from many childhood days spent playing with my cousins he would shed his fishing clothes down there, shower and change before he appeared in the kitchen.

Aunt Sharon pulled a loaf out of the breadbox. It was double-wrapped in plastic wrap covered by aluminum foil. Aunt Sharon was a great believer in wrapping things as tightly and redundantly as possible. I knew what it was before she began to peel away the layers. My Aunt Sharon's justifiably famous banana bread. She cut me a slice without asking if I wanted one and poured me cup of coffee and put milk in it. How had she remembered?

The banana bread was equal in every way to the sense memory I had of it. It was rich and spicy and moist with the crunch of walnuts adding to the texture. It took me immediately to my childhood afternoons in that house, my cousin Robbie bursting in on Francie and me as we were deep in some Barbie-related scenario. When the screaming and fighting got to be too much, Aunt Sharon would call us down for a snack. I hadn't spoken to Francie in . . . I couldn't remember. How could I have let it go so long?

Aunt Sharon and I caught up on my cousins' lives.

Francie was a teacher like her mother. She taught high school English in her North Jersey town. Her husband worked on Wall Street. I was startled to hear her girls were four and six. I'd lost track of the time. My cousin Robbie was in Los Angeles working construction during the day and playing guitar and singing the songs he wrote in clubs at night. When Aunt Sharon heard Uncle Bob's heavy tread on the wooden cellar stairs, she hurried through her report on their son, closing the subject before the basement door opened into the kitchen.

"Julia!" Uncle Bob boomed. "To what do we owe the pleasure?"

"I was in town." (True.) "It's a relatively quiet time at the business." (Also true. But not the truth.)

"How's your mother?"

"She's good." None of my father's family had known what to make of it when the eldest son had married a summer person who lived on a private island. And my mother, raised by her widowed father and a succession of housekeepers, hadn't known what to make of his family and their noisy and unvarnished opinions about how everyone should live. "You know what you should do—" But over time, as families do, they accepted one another. My mother loved my cousins and her in-laws. She never forgot a birthday, graduation, or anniversary.

Uncle Bob poured coffee into a mug that said, WORLD'S BEST GRANDAD. "Good for her." He sat heavily at the round fake-wood kitchen table. "So what's new, kiddo? What's happening?"

My opening. "I'm here in Damariscotta visiting a friend of my boyfriend Chris Durand's."

"Your mother mentioned him," Aunt Sharon said.

"*Quite a while ago*." Did she say the italics, or did I alone hear them? This was not the conversational track I wanted to go down.

"His friend's name is Andie Greatorex. She owns Great River Oysters. Do you know her?"

"'Course," my uncle said.

"I heard what happened to her," Aunt Sharon added. "Such a shame. She's lucky she wasn't hurt."

"She wasn't hurt badly, but she lost a huge amount of oyster spat. Have you heard any rumors about who might have done it?"

"No." My uncle didn't leave room for argument, even if my aunt had been inclined to gossip.

I pushed a little harder. "I heard some of the lobstermen on the river are pretty upset because she's applied for a bigger leasehold."

"Of course we are," Bob said. "Pretty soon there'll be nothing but aquaculture out there. They're pushing us lobstermen out. We're the biggest fishery left in this state. We should be taken care of, not moved aside. And the state doesn't charge them oyster farmers nearly what those leases are worth. They're giving them away."

I thought that was pretty rich, considering the lobstermen paid nothing for the places they set their traps. They were highly territorial, but trap placement was governed by where you lived and by seniority. God help the newbie who put a trap down next to or on top of some old lobsterman's, or worse, got it into the water before he did and stole one of his spots.

"They're having a hearing about her lease application this Friday night. I'll be there speaking against it and so will a lot of others."

"Is anyone more upset than anyone else? Anyone especially angry? Maybe they lost their bottom to a lease or fear they will."

I'd gone too far. My uncle flushed bright red. "What are you implying?"

"I'm not implying anything. I'm curious."

"No lobsterman robbed Andie; I guarantee it." When he saw my skeptical look, he added, "For one thing, there's not a lobsterman on this peninsula who can keep his mouth shut. If someone did it, he'd be telling the tale to anyone who would listen."

"Even though it's a felony?"

"When did that ever stop tongues from wagging?" He laughed and my aunt laughed, so I laughed, and the tension was broken.

"Okay, not the assault and robbery," I conceded. "But what about minor stuff, just to let the farmers know you guys aren't happy?"

My uncle sat back in his chair. "Like?"

"Cutting buoy lines, turning over cages."

He laughed again. "No lobsterman would bother with that penny-ante stuff." He waved a big, calloused hand, dismissing it.

I knew better. Lobstermen were capable of that kind of mayhem and more. They did it to each other—cutting traplines, deliberately tangling gear—when territorial disputes broke out. But I didn't argue. "Do you have any thoughts about who else might have robbed Andie?" I asked while everyone was in such a good mood.

"There's other oyster farms on this river. Some of those farmers aren't too happy about Great River's proposed expansion. They feel like they're going to be squeezed out."

"Anyone in particular?"

"Ken Farrow. He's the newest farm on the river. I hear he's struggling. He's undercapitalized and his leasehold is too small to yield a profit. If Andie Greatorex's new lease blocks any hope he has of expansion, he might get pretty heated up. My money's on him."

The conversation moved on. The arthritis in Aunt Sharon's hands was bothering her, but she had two more years to teach at Busman's Harbor Elementary to maximize her pension. Uncle Bob was having problems with his prostate, "Not anything I want to discuss."

As I got ready to go, Aunt Sharon triple-wrapped the rest of the banana bread and handed it to me.

"I couldn't."

"You can and you will."

They walked me to the door and each of them hugged me. "Give our love to your mother, and your sister and her family," Aunt Sharon said.

"Don't be such a stranger," Uncle Bob added and closed the door.

Ken Farrow's oyster farm, Midden Bay Oyster Farm, was on the same side of the river as my aunt and uncle's house, but farther from town. As I aimed the Subaru toward his location, I had the sensation I was traveling in a big circle. Mack Owen had pointed me to the lobstermen in the person of my uncle. My uncle had pointed me toward the other oyster farmers in the person of Ken Farrow.

Still, talking to Farrow made sense. I needed to find out what the other farmers thought about Andie, Great River, and her lease application. And I was mindful of what Andie told me. Only another oyster farmer with a system to care for the baby oysters could get any value from the theft. I had no idea if he would be at his farm, but I had no other way to reach him, so I took the chance.

I turned off onto a private road and followed it to a wooden two-story house. In the distance, down a green lawn I could see a simple dock and a small shed. A boat with an outboard motor was tied up at the dock, which gave me hope Farrow was around.

The setup at Midden Bay was quite different from Andie's place. It lacked her retail store, shipping barn, picnic area and elaborate dock complex on the river. I couldn't tell if the white house with the deep porch was a residence or had been converted to offices for the farm. I couldn't locate a bell, so I rapped on the door and called, "Anybody here?" No answer. All the windows were closed against the cool May breeze and I wasn't sure anyone had heard me.

My third set of knocks produced a result. "All right, all right! I'm coming." Through the window in the door I watched a man come toward me from somewhere in the back of the house. An aged golden retriever trailed behind him, not barking, moving slowly. If the man was Ken Farrow, he was older than I expected for someone who had recently started a business, especially a business that wouldn't pay off for a while. He had a shock of pure white hair on his head, but his brows were dark, almost black. The skin on his face, arms, and the legs that showed beneath his cargo shorts, was very tan. He was tall and lean, exactly the physical description Andie had given for her attacker, though he stooped slightly as he walked. Andie thought the robber moved like a younger man, but could she really tell? She had been taken by surprise and the attack was over in seconds. But then, if she was right that the robber had been hired by someone else, Ken Farrow's physique didn't matter.

The door opened. "Sorry. We don't do retail here. No tours of the farm. Nothing open to the public." Up close I could see he was younger than I had at first supposed. Early fifties maybe.

"Mr. Farrow?" I stuck out my hand. "I'm Julia Snowden."

He took the hand and shook. "Snowden? You one of those clambake Snowdens?"

"I am. My parents founded the company and I run it now."

"Ken Farrow, owner of Midden Bay Oyster Farm. What can I do for you?" His tone was open and not hostile. Evidently my bona fides as a local and a business owner made me much more acceptable than some random tourist From Away standing on his porch.

"I wonder if we could talk for a minute." I purposefully didn't state my reason for desiring a conversation. I didn't think it would persuade him.

Apparently, I didn't need to explain myself, because he nodded and said, "C'mon in."

I followed him inside. The house was barebones, minimal furniture in the living room—no rug, nothing but paper shades on the windows. But it did appear he was living there. He brought me into the kitchen were a few crusts of a sandwich sat on a plate on the drainboard next to an empty glass showing a tiny bit of milk.

The dog followed, sniffing at my hands. "Don't mind Red," Farrow said. "He's pretty much blind and almost

entirely deaf. Dogs get most of their info from smell anyway, but he's particularly dependent on his nose." Red
gave one last sniff and limped away. Evidently, I was
okay.

Farrow sat me at the table and offered coffee or tea as
a good host would. I was vibrating like a tuning fork from
the strong cup at my aunt's house, so I refused politely.
He took a chair. "How can I help you?"

"My boyfriend is good friends with Andie Greatorex,"
I started.

"Ayup," he said, waiting for more.

"Did you hear what happened to her?"

"I did. It's a shame." His light blue eyes drilled into
mine. His were somehow both mesmerizing and a little
menacing.

"Andie's trying to understand what happened to her.
She's asked me to help."

"The police have already been here looking for upwellers." His tone was sharp.

"Looking *for* upwellers?" I was confused. Shouldn't
they be looking *in* upwellers for the missing seed? But
then how on earth would they identify the seed as stolen?
I supposed they could check with the limited number of
hatcheries to see who had made purchases recently and
figure out if someone had oyster spat who shouldn't. It
was an approach that confirmed what Andie believed.
The police were pursuing the crime as a robbery, something taken for its value.

"But I surprised them," Farrow continued. "I don't
have upwellers. I will eventually, but for now I buy my
stock from other farms when the oysters are ready to be
put in the cages. For all I know some of those oyster ba-

bies that got stolen from Great River were eventually going to be headed over here. Why would I steal them if I can't keep them?"

Why indeed. "Andie told me she has had to deal with petty harassments, people cutting the lines to her buoys or turning cages over. Have you experienced anything like that?"

"We all have."

"Have you noticed it's been happening more lately?"

"Can't say as I have," he answered. "You should know, though, there's a debate among the farmers about whether it's deliberate or simple negligence. Lazy boaters not looking where they're going, lobstermen dropping traps too close and then cutting our lines to disentangle them. That sort of thing."

"What do you think, sabotage or negligence?"

"Couldn't say. Sabotage is a strong word."

"I would say so too, except Andie was assaulted."

"She thinks they're connected?" His dark brows drew together in a frown.

"Andie doesn't think the assault and robbery was for gain," I told him. "She thinks it was intended to intimidate her. That's why I wanted to talk to her fellow farmers. Can you think of a reason someone might want to hurt Andie?"

Farrow sat back, letting his long, tan arms hang at his sides. "That's quite an accusation."

"I didn't mean it to be. It's a theory, nothing more."

He shifted on the hard kitchen chair and put his arms back on the table. "I suppose you've heard about this lease application?"

"I have."

"If Andie gets the lease, she'll own the biggest operation on the river. Plenty of people are opposed to that."

"Like you?"

"My leasehold isn't even big enough to support a farm that can make a profit. I'll need to expand, and soon. I have two concerns about Andie's application. One is the state approves her application, and then decides the river has too much area under lease and denies any future leases. And two, even if that doesn't happen, I'm worried Andie's application has become such a rallying point for people opposed to more aquaculture that the public pressure will be so strong the state will refuse any more leases. Either way, I'm toast."

I understood his concerns, but were they enough to cause the mild-mannered, if slightly curmudgeonly, man in front of me to hire someone to commit a violent crime? It seemed doubtful, though he clearly thought his livelihood was threatened by Andie's proposed expansion. "You feel strongly," I said. "Can you think of anyone else who feels strongly?"

"Strongly enough to knock Andie down and rob her?"

"Andie doesn't believe the assailant was someone she knows. She thinks the perpetrator was hired, acting on someone else's behalf."

"Does she now?" Farrow rose from his chair. "Come see my operation," he said.

He led me down an expanse of lawn toward his dock. He strolled slowly and it took me a moment to realize he was setting the pace so Red could keep up with us.

"How did you get in the oyster farming business?" I asked.

"I had a lobster boat over in Muscongus Bay," he said.

"The handwriting is on the wall. Landings are bigger than ever, but the Gulf of Maine is warming faster than any other body of water on earth save one. As the lobsters follow the colder water soon there will only be two choices: haul out deeper or move to Canada. Neither one appealed to me so I decided to try my hand at aquaculture. I sold my boat and gear, gave up my lobstering license and bought this leasehold from a guy who never got any oysters planted on the bottom." Farrow made a noise halfway between a laugh and a grunt. "I should have known."

Farrow had gone all in on the oyster farm. It was true what he said, the water around us was warming rapidly. But the move seemed precipitous. Plenty of lobstermen were still landing plenty of lobsters. At his age, Farrow might have been able to ride a lobstering career out to his natural retirement.

"How has it been for you?" I asked.

This time he did laugh. "It's been an education is all I can say. They say when a lobsterman takes up aquaculture it's like when a hunter/gatherer becomes a farmer. It's an enormous cultural change, but one you'd undertake to survive." He paused. "But I'll harvest my first crop this summer. That will be a celebration, let me tell you. I'm already lining up restaurant accounts."

I was surprised my uncle hadn't mentioned Ken Farrow was a former lobsterman. But perhaps even though it was on the same peninsula, Muscongus Bay was far enough away that Uncle Bob didn't consider Farrow a member of his crew.

We reached the dock. A sorting shed stood on the landward end of it. It was newly built and still gave off a powerful smell of recently sawn wood. It was much smaller than the one at Andie's. A single glass-paned window was next to its door. No more than two people could work in there, three max. There was no sign of upwellers, as Farrow had said. Farrow's home and dock were directly across from the Great River operation. Three people were on Andie's dock by the sorting shed. The river was wide at that point and the figures looked tiny on the other side. I assumed one was Andie and the others were her employees who sorted the oysters but couldn't be sure.

"There's my cages out there." Farrow pointed to three neat rows of oyster cages strung together about thirty yards from the dock. Indeed, it wasn't many compared to Great River. "See that house there?"

I followed the finger on his left hand to the imposing, shingle-styled house next to Andie's property on the other side of the woods. "Andie's neighbors," I said. "She bought the farm property and her cottage from them."

"Right," Farrow said. "The property belongs to the Kirwins. That house has been there since the late 1800s, but the Kirwins have owned that land since the 1770s. They ran their shipbuilding operation there. From 1779 onward there were dozens of shipyards on this river. They built more than four hundred ships, including five-masted schooners, brigs, barks, and sloops. The Kirwins built a good healthy number of those. They made a fortune. But then, after the Civil War, the railroad came in and the shipbuilding business declined. The Kirwins took off for richer, more powerful places, Wall Street, Washington DC, San Francisco. John Bullard Kirwin removed the ship works, tore down the colonial home that stood on the lot and built a summer house. The family is still there.

"Pinney Kirwin is the senior Kirwin now. She hates the oyster farms. Says the cages look like old tires floating in her river. Spoils her view. She has some notion that the oysters pollute the river, when in point of fact they clean it.

"She has her nerve calling us polluters. At their peak, the shipyards and their sawmills dumping sawdust killed the river. Took almost a hundred years to clean it up. At one point there wasn't a single tree along the banks, all cut down for shipbuilding. They're the polluters, not us."

It was hard to imagine the banks of the Damariscotta denuded. There were trees wherever there wasn't a lawn, house, or road. But almost all the woods in New England were second growth, third even. The land was cleared aggressively for farms, ships, and paper.

"This woman, Pinney Kirwin, opposes Andie's lease application?" I asked.

"With a passion. I was in Mack's Oyster Shack last Friday for local's night. Pinney was buttonholing everyone there to make sure that they'd be at the hearing to speak out against Andie."

"That's a long way from assault."

"It is. But you said Andie believes it was someone who was hired to do it. Maybe it got out of hand. Pinney Kirwin has the money, she has the motive, and she's ruthless. If I was Andie, or the police, I'd be looking there."

The circle continued.

The driveway into Pinney Kirwin's property was made of crushed seashells, a sure sign of a summer residence because it would be horrible to plow. The other tipoff was that the house had a name, not a number, out on the River Road. The Chandlery, it was called.

I pulled up at the front of the house, which is to say the

back. When a house faced a body of water, the side of the house facing the street was the back, the side facing the water was the front. Or so I had always been taught.

Chris was of another opinion. He believed the side of the house that faced the street was always the front. This made for many lively, funny arguments as we'd driven around Busman's Harbor, especially because most of the summer houses Chris took care of were on the water.

The door to the main entrance to the Kirwin house was open. A wooden screen door, its frame painted the same brown as the rest of the house trim, let in the breeze. I thought the weather was still a touch cold to leave the door open, but to each his own.

There was no sign of a car, but there was a large garage on one side of the drive, so Pinney Kirwin might be home. The doorbell gave a deep and satisfying pong. "Hello!" I called through the screen.

"Coming! Just a moment." For a disembodied voice, the tone was firm.

While I waited, I looked around. The place wasn't as foreboding as it had appeared from across the river. Up close, the shingles looked rough, the trim in need of refreshing. But the flowerpots on either side of the front steps were filled with colorful coleuses and the beds beside the house with newly planted pink and white impatiens.

"May I help you?"

I jumped. I'd been so busy taking in the details of the house I'd momentarily forgotten I was waiting for anyone.

"Ms. Kirwin?" I had no doubt the woman dressed in the pink cotton skirt and coordinated flower-printed top was Pinney Kirwin. The ash-blonde hair held back by a pink headband fell to gentle, upturned curls on her shoulders in a style my mother would have called a flip.

"I am she. And you are?"

"Julia Snowden."

Her slightly puzzled look was replaced by a smile. "From the Snowden Family Clambake? I know your mother. I've been to the clambake many times. It's a highlight when we have houseguests who've come to Maine for the first time. How can I help you, Julia?"

She must have thought I was there on behalf of a local charity or some similarly worthy mission. "I'm here about your neighbor, Andie Greatorex."

Her suspicious look returned. "What about her?" She hadn't opened the screen door.

I looked down at my jeans. I was glad I'd left the flannel shirt and work boots at home. "It will take a minute to explain. May I come in?"

Pinney Kirwin hesitated ever so slightly and then opened the screen. I couldn't be a crazed killer if she knew my mother, could I? I followed her through a large entrance hall into the living room beyond it. The outside wall was lined with windows framing spectacular river views. Reflections of the blue, blue sky, and the bright spring leaves on the trees were reflected in the water. Andie's and Ken Farrow's oyster cages bobbed up and down.

"Sit, please." Ms. Kirwin gestured toward a set of two chintz couches facing one another in the center of the large, well-proportioned room. Like the home's facade, the chintz was faded but otherwise beautiful. I chose one of the couches and she sat across from me. There was a large stone fireplace on the wall opposite the windows with built-in shelves on either side of it. On the shelves, Chinese vases, commemorative silver plates, crystal candlesticks and all manner of antique knick-knacks were grouped by color, size, and design for maximum visual impact.

And old, primitive-style painting of a shipyard hung over the fireplace. A sign on one of the shipyard buildings in the picture said, "Kirwin's." There was a sawmill, a brickworks, a sail-making shed with its doors open to show the sails inside, and an elaborate dock system with several sailing ships in various states of construction. Behind the business was a magnificent lawn leading to a colonial house, the predecessor presumably of the one I was in now. In the distance you could also see Andie's cottage and the shipping barn, used as a stable. Kirwin's Shipyard extended along the entire riverfront captured in the painting, from one end of the colonial house lawn to past where Andie's dock complex stood now.

"What an interesting painting." I gambled it was the absolute right thing to say.

Pinney stood. "My ancestors put this town on the map. The Kirwins were the most productive, highest quality builders of ships on the Damariscotta." She turned to me. "The Kirwins and people like us," she graciously allowed, "built this country."

I happened to believe that lots of additional people built the country, including the people who worked in those shipyards, and those who sailed the ships, and those who waited for them, and the slaves who undoubtedly arrived on some of those ships and so many others. But I smiled and gritted my teeth. She sat back down, my history lesson apparently over.

"Ms. Kirwin," I began.

"Pinney, please. I was born Penelope, but everyone calls me Pinney. You said this was about my neighbor."

"You may have heard that Andie was assaulted and robbed."

"I did indeed."

"Did the police talk to you about it?"

"Gracious, no. Why would they?" Pinney looked to be in her early sixties. She was made up even though it appeared she was home alone. Every hair stayed in place, as if afraid to stray. I had a lifetime of dealing with women like Pinney. They organized parties, charity functions, and other occasions and brought their guests to our clambake. These women demanded quality. They demanded to be heard and demanded everyone—their guests, our other guests, our employees—be on their best behavior. They had unwavering beliefs about how everyone and everything should be.

My mother could have been a woman like Pinney. She was raised for it. If you substituted the ice business for shipbuilding, my mother's family history was similar to the Kirwins'. Windsholme, the soon-to-be renovated mansion on Morrow Island where we ran our clambakes was built in the same era as the house I was in now. But at the age of twenty-two, my mother had taken a hard-left turn. Instead of the doctor, lawyer, or banker her college professor father had expected, she had married the son of a lobsterman. The money in her family had all been gone for decades by that point. The age of making fortunes by harvesting ice from the rivers of Maine and shipping it to New York City, New Orleans, Havana, and Mumbai was long over. Now, in the fall, winter, and spring my mother wore a smock and name tag and managed the day shift at

Linens and Pantries, the big box store in Topsham. She'd never expressed a single regret.

"Andie said the thief escaped into the woods between your properties," I told Pinney, "so I thought the police might have come by to ask if you'd seen anyone."

"They haven't and I didn't." She wrapped her arms around herself and gave an exaggerated shudder. "It's terrible something like this could happen in our little town. So frightening."

Not too frightening evidently, since she'd left her door wide open while she'd been on the other side of the house, with all the treasures in this room and nothing but a thin screen to protect them. Andie's thief had already proved he didn't mind kicking people to the ground. Perhaps he was willing to do worse. But people like Pinney weren't easily frightened.

"What I don't understand is why *you're* talking to me," Pinney said.

There was the rub. "Andie is a friend. She's concerned the police don't understand the motive for the theft. They're distracted by the value of what was stolen and are viewing it as a simple robbery."

"What does Ms. Greatorex view the motive as?" The air in the room had grown decidedly chillier. I looked out the big windows to see if a cloud had passed over the sun, but blue sky still danced on the water.

"Andie is concerned that the assault and robbery were intended to damage her financially in order to put her out of business. Or to dissuade her from pursuing another leasehold for her farm."

"And she sent you in my direction, did she?" The temperature plummeted further.

"No, no, no. I came here all on my own. You're a

neighbor and I thought perhaps you could shed some light on the incident."

"I will shed some light, as you say. And then you will leave." She paused, but only for a second. "I am opposed with every fiber of my being to any further expansion of the oyster farms on the river. The cages are unsightly, and I fear the density of the oysters on the river bottom will foul it and chase out other living things. To be clear, I am not opposed to Ms. Greatorex's expansion specifically, though I do wish I had a neighbor with a more refined property, more commensurate with mine. I am opposed to all expansion anywhere on the river. I will be at the meeting on Friday evening and I will be speaking out forcefully. Further, and I do not believe that I have to say this, I am not a criminal. I do not knock people down and I do not take things that do not belong to me. Period. Ever."

She stood and I followed her lead. "I don't know what you're playing at, but I would urge you to give it up and return your attention to your family's very fine business."

She walked me out and closed both the screen and heavy wooden door behind me without saying good-bye.

CHAPTER FIVE

I had half an hour on the drive back to Busman's Harbor to think about what I'd learned. Andie had been unable to conceive of any of the people I'd spoken to hurting her, and after meeting them, I felt the same way. Mack Owen had moved on from any resentments that might have resulted from his breakup, both personal and professional, with Andie. He had a wife and kids and an apparently successful business he loved. Ken Farrow was a nice enough man trying to make a career change in late mid-life. It was a struggle no doubt. He seemed worried but not angry.

I could see Pinney Kirwin bashing Andie over the head with an umbrella while tossing off a cutting remark, but I didn't see her hiring a thug to steal thirty-five thousand dollars' worth of oyster seed. How would she even find a thug? The criminals in Pinney's circle probably tended more toward insider trading and tax evasion.

And my Uncle Bob was, well, my uncle. He might be a bit grumpy at little kids who ran around his house shrieking, or teenagers who were still in bed at noon, but he was also generous and loyal. The best kind of uncle. I couldn't see him getting angry enough to commit assault and robbery, even at a remove.

It was five-thirty. I had spent a day on Andie's problem, and I had gotten nowhere. The job applications for the clambake waited for my attention. If I didn't get to them soon, every single person in the pile would already have a job. I'd done what I could with what little Andie had been willing to give me. Tomorrow I would be back at my desk.

The question for me still was, who knew Andie would be at her truck with that valuable cargo at that moment? It led back to her employees and the employees at the hatchery. The police would have figured that out. I hoped they were having better luck than I was.

On my way into town, I stopped at Hannaford to pick up milk. Thursday's edition of the *Busman's Harbor Gazette* was already in the bin ready for the next morning. Andie's photo and story were on the front page. The idea you could steal thirty-five thousand dollars by grabbing two standard-sized pails made for compelling reading. Now everyone would know what had happened.

I left my car in its bay in Mom's garage and walked up the harbor hill to the studio apartment over Gus's restaurant, which Chris and I shared. The place was empty when I got inside. Gus only served breakfast and lunch. I trudged upstairs. I put the milk and banana bread in the fridge, confident my aunt's triple wrapping job would prevent it from drying out.

A text showed up on my screen. **CHRIS: DINNER AT CROWLEY'S? I'M HERE NOW**

He didn't have to ask twice. Even though we'd already been out to lunch, once the clambake opened for the season it would be months before we had a lunch or dinner out, or even together. I grabbed the Snowden Family tote bag I used as a handbag and headed out the door.

Chris was already seated at a table for two along the wall in the main room of the restaurant. He had a Sam Adams bottle in front of him.

"Great idea," I said.

"I thought so. How did your afternoon go?"

I filled him in on my progress or lack thereof.

"What'll you do next?" he asked.

I shifted in my seat and looked into his green eyes. "I'm not sure how into this Andie is. She may have accepted my help to please you. She didn't give me anything to work with."

From his reaction, I could tell Chris wasn't happy, but he didn't press me to continue. When our server came around, I ordered a glass of Malbec and we both chose burgers because the ones Crowley's served were heaven. The waitress was new and didn't look old enough to serve alcohol. She smiled at Chris and went off to put in our order and get my wine.

"So tell me," I started, "What's the big secret with your poker games?"

He put his glass down. "What does that mean?"

"You kept me from your family and didn't tell me a thing about them and it turned out there was a *big* secret. Since you've never introduced me to your poker friends, I'm assuming there's a big secret there, too."

"Julia." He spoke my name then stopped. For more than two years his standard response to all inquiries had been, "My family isn't like yours." I'd known some of his history. That he hadn't gone to college even though he'd had a full scholarship. That he'd bought his cabin from his father. That his parents lived in Florida. But then the rest of it came out, an older brother in prison, a sister he was estranged from, a mother with a debilitating, ultimately fatal and heritable disease. A disease he'd never been tested for.

We'd gotten through the set of revelations and events I thought of collectively as "the mess." Mostly because I truly believed the reason he hadn't told me the truth about his family wasn't about me or our relationship. It was because he couldn't think about it too closely or for too long or form the words to tell me. Until he had to. We had gone on from there, happily I thought. But we were both still raw around the edges.

I could see where this fun night out was going. "Do you play naked?" I teased. "Or do you bet your cars or something weirder? What's the deal? Spill."

Chris relaxed visibly. "I tell you about poker," he said.

"You do. Sometimes you say, 'I won.' And sometimes you say, 'I lost.'"

"That's not true." He smiled. "Sometimes I say, 'I killed,' and sometimes I say, 'I got killed.'" He shifted in his chair. "Honestly, you've never shown a lot of interest. Are you freaking out because Andie is a girl?"

"I'm freaking out because I didn't realize Andie is a girl, and that makes me wonder what else I may not realize."

"Nothing. I can't think of a single other thing that would surprise you. It's a group of friends I've played cards with during the off-season for fifteen years. People have come and gone. They move out or end up on a night shift or have kids like Mack did. But others move back home, or a friend invites a friend and the game keeps going. Andie, Sam, and I go back to the beginning. That's it. That's all of it."

"But why have you never introduced me? They know I exist. That's clear. Andie even knew I'd worked with the police."

Chris put his hand over mine. "Of course they know you exist. I talk about you all the time. You're the most important person in my life. More important than anything."

"But why have you never introduced me? Except to Sam because you had to because you work for him here."

"I don't know, Julia. It's not like I purposefully kept you away. It's a poker game. Unless you were going to play, how would that even work? Would you come in, curtsey, and leave? Because that would be weird."

"And now it's weirder that they've never met me." I wasn't going to concede the point so easily. "You told Andie about your family."

"Is that what this is about?" He smiled and the lines around his deep green eyes crinkled. "Andie lost her mom a few years ago. It had only ever been the two of them. She took it hard. She knew I didn't have anybody, so she reached out to me. She and Mack were breaking up around that time. She wanted someone to talk to. I couldn't let her assume I was an orphan like she was. It made me feel like a fraud. So I told her about my family." He rested his elbows on the table, bringing his face toward mine. "That's all. That's it."

The young server delivered our burgers and I was grateful for the interruption. Chris and I moved on to other topics. Work, plans, people we knew, the usual couple things. When we were done, I excused myself and headed to the ladies' room.

Crowley's was a big, old waterfront warehouse that contained multiple noisy rooms. In the summer there was live entertainment and the decibel level was insane. The restrooms were inconveniently located as far from the bar and main dining room as possible. I followed the well-known path through the restaurant on autopilot.

That's when I saw her. Lacey Brenneman, Andie Greatorex's disgruntled ex-employee. She was at a table in the farthest room. If she saw me, she didn't remember me. She'd been focused on Andie, and maybe a little on Josh, during her tirade that morning.

Even more intriguing, was her dinner companion. A guy, about her age, dressed all in black. He was lean like Andie had said her attacker was and he'd be tall when he stood up. His back was to me. I couldn't see his face. But then Andie hadn't either.

Heart thumping, I went to the restroom to try to figure out what to do. I hadn't brought my tote bag, so I didn't have my phone to take a photo. In the end I skittled back to my seat, walking head down against the far wall of the room where Lacey and her companion were seated. I didn't sit down when I got our table. I scrabbled through the tote bag looking for my phone.

"What's up?" Chris looked worried.

"I saw that unhappy employee of Andie's in the other room here. She's with a guy who looks exactly how Andie described her assailant. I want to get a photo and send it to Andie to see if she recognizes him."

"Andie only saw him for a few seconds and didn't see his face. You're going to send her a photo of him sitting in a chair?"

I sat down heavily. "You're right. That makes no sense. I got carried away because I thought after a fruitless day I'd discovered something."

"You should wait until he leaves. Take a photo of him walking. And take one of his back, since that's mostly what Andie saw and from low down, because she was on the ground, looking up."

"Brilliant. Switch places with me. I'll recognize them."

We changed chairs.

"Did they have their entrees?" Chris asked.

"Yes, but there was a lot of food on their plates."

"Okay," he said. "We wait. Dessert?"

Crowley's had a brownie sundae I could never turn down, so we put an order in for one and waited. We'd consumed as much of the gooey deliciousness as we could when I spotted Lacey and her dinner companion walking across the main room toward the front door.

They were going to pass right by us. The light wasn't great, but I took a couple of quick photos of the guy from the front, his face and his full body. He towered over Lacey. Then I tossed my phone to Chris who took several photos of the man's back, including some from down around the floor to show what the guy would like if you were on the ground.

I scrolled through the photos. Some were blurry, but most weren't bad. I texted them to Andie along with an explanation. **Saw this guy having dinner with Lacey Brenneman. Your assailant?**

I was excited and expected to hear right back, but my phone didn't ring. We paid our bill and walked out into the night, hoping and waiting.

Andie called about a half an hour after we got home. "Julia?" She sounded excited, breathless.

"Did you see them?" I was eager for her response to the photos.

"That's what I'm calling about. But how do you know?"

"How do I know what?" I was confused. "I sent them to you."

"What?"

Clearly, we were talking at cross purposes. "What are you talking about?"

"I got a ransom note."

Now it was my turn to say, "WHAT?"

"I went out to pick up some takeout for dinner and when I got back there was a note under the door at my house. Half a sheet of torn paper. It said, 'I have your oysters. Leave five thousand in cash in a manila envelope in your mailbox before ten tomorrow morning and we'll leave instructions for their safe return. A friend.' Julia, what should I do?"

"You should call the police."

"I did. They're coming to pick up the note."

"Is it printed like from a computer or cut-out letters or what?" Was that still a thing?

"It's handwritten. I'll take a photo of it before the police get here and text it to you. But what I meant was, should I give this person five thousand dollars?"

That didn't sound like a good idea. "What did the police say?"

"Not to do anything until they got here, but I have a feeling they're going to tell me not to give money to a criminal. But if I could have my seed back it would be worth it."

"Then I guess you should ask for proof of life," I said, only half in jest. "Do you have five thousand in cash?"

"I have whatever's locked in the cash drawer at the store and whatever my ATM twenty-four-hour withdrawal limit is," Andie said. "So probably not. Maybe I could get to the bank first thing in the morning."

"Do whatever the cops tell you to," I said.

"Okay." It wasn't the advice she wanted. "What did you think I was talking about when you called?"

"I sent you a few photos of Lacey Brenneman's boyfriend. I assume he's her boyfriend. They were having dinner tonight at Crowley's. He's tall like you described, not an ounce of fat on him."

"What time did you see them?" Andie asked.

"I spotted them around seven-fifteen. They left around eight."

"I left to pick up my dinner at seven and got back at seven-thirty. It's half an hour from Busman's Harbor to Damariscotta. It couldn't have been them who left the note."

I thought for a moment. "The ransom note probably has nothing to do with the robbery. Your story was in the *Gazette* tonight, so everybody in the area knows about it. Mostly likely, someone's trying to take advantage of your situation. Whoever it is doesn't seem too experienced with blackmail. Telling you to leave the money in your mailbox. No warning not to talk to the cops. No photo of your seed. It's hard to take it seriously. I'm more worried about something else." I tried to keep my voice calm, but the words came out too quickly. "How did whoever left the note know exactly when you'd be gone? That's a really tight window. They must be watching you. Stay on the line with me until the cops get there."

"Julia, you're freaking me out." Andie had been cool and determined when she'd described being shoved to the ground and robbed. Now she sounded shaky. The cumulative effect was getting to her.

"Call a friend. Have them stay with you tonight or go to their house."

"No. I'm fine. I'd be mortified." The firmness was back in her voice.

"Chris and I will come. We'll leave right now."

"No!"

"Andie, someone is watching you."

"Well, whoever they are, they're gone now. Three cop cars just pulled into the drive, lights and sirens blazing."

I could hear the sirens through the phone. That's not how I would have picked up a ransom note from a victim, but small-town cops don't have a lot to do. Any hint of excitement attracted them like flies.

"They're at the door, or some of them are. I see flashlights all over my yard. I have to go. Come in the morning, please and talk this through with me."

"Look at the photos I sent. I'll be there in the morning."

CHAPTER SIX

In the morning, as I drove to Great River Oyster Farm, I turned the idea of the ransom note over in my head. Was it connected to the theft or was it a random individual taking advantage of the publicity about Andie's stolen oyster seed? For that matter, was the petty vandalism Andie had described a part of the pattern? Vandalism felt different than assault and robbery, which felt different again from seed-napping and a ransom demand. But could three different individuals be arrayed against Andie? The controversy over her lease expansion aside, she seemed like a perfectly nice person, a businesswoman who provided jobs and revenue for the community.

The farm shop wasn't yet open for the day, but once I'd parked my car I could see Josh moving inside. I knocked.

"Andie around? I'm Julia."

"Hi. I remember you." He pushed his long bangs out of his eyes with a hand. "Andie went out early harvesting like she does every day. Did she know you were coming?"

"She knew I'd be here this morning, but we didn't set a time."

"She'll probably be in soon if she's not back already. Your best bet is to go down to the dock to wait."

I thanked him and walked down the steep road to the riverfront. When Andie's dock complex came into view, her boat was nowhere to be seen. The day was sunny and warm for May, but not at all hot. The sound of the pumps pushing water through the upwellers kept up a steady but not unpleasant thrum. In the sorting shed, everything was neat as a pin, exactly as it had been the day before. Plastic crates were piled along one wall. The white pails with GREAT RIVER stenciled on them were stacked in the corner.

I wasn't sure how long I should hang around. Josh expected Andie back soon. I was anxious to talk about the ransom note and see if she recognized the guy in the photos. I walked to the end of the dock, staring out along the river. If Andie came close enough to see me there, I could wave to attract her attention.

I stood on the end of the dock, gazing at the river. Sleek sailboats bobbed at their moorings. The oyster cages moved gently with the current. On a small island, an eagle sat in a nest at the top of a pine tree. Houses peeked out here and there among green treetops. Across the river, Ken Farrow was out on his dock, readying his boat as if to go out. Red stood watching, his long tail oc-

casionally fluttering in anticipation of the ride. At my
aunt and uncle's dock, *My Sharona* was gone. Uncle Bob
was probably farther down the river, closer to the sea,
dropping his lobster traps into position, getting ready for
the season.

It was all so quiet and peaceful.

I don't know what made me look down.

It took me a moment to comprehend what I was looking at. Then I did. Andie's body bobbed in the water at
the end of the dock, looking as peaceful as the rest of the
scene.

"Yikes!" I jumped backwards involuntarily and almost
fell over. I took a deep breath that failed to steady me and
lay down on the dock. I stretched to see if I could pull her
out of the water, even though I knew it was pointless to
try to save her. She was facedown, the end of her ponytail
fanned out on the surface. Her feet were tangled in bright
blue netting that was secured to the dock. I reached for
her black wet-suited arm and pulled.

She rolled toward me, hazel eyes open and unseeing,
an oyster knife with a blue handle protruding from her
neck.

I sat in the back of an ambulance in the parking area by
the shop, wrapped in a blanket though I wasn't injured
and hadn't gotten wet. The nice EMT who had helped me
was worried about shock and I could see her point.

I'd left Andie in the water. I couldn't lift her out, and
she was beyond saving. I called 911 and reported what
I'd found. Then I walked back up the hill to break the
news to Josh and direct the police cars. I called Chris and

then I waited. It didn't take long for the first responders to arrive.

A Damariscotta policeman who introduced himself as Sergeant Dundee asked me the basics. When did I arrive? What did I see? What did I do? I told him everything I could while it was still fresh in my memory. Then he returned to the dock and left me alone in the back of the ambulance.

My phone rang somewhere in the depths of my tote bag. I found it in time to answer the call, just. It was Chris.

"They won't let me up the farm road."

"Tell them you've come to pick me up."

"I did. The cop here said they'd bring you down when you could leave."

"I'm not sure I can drive." The Subaru wasn't far away. It looked alien, not like my comfortable, beloved car.

"Don't worry. I'll wait. No matter how long." He said it with such tenderness.

"I'm sorry. I know she was your friend. I really liked her." My voice squeaked up at the end of the sentence. I clamped my mouth shut and fought for control.

"You take care of you for now. We'll talk about Andie later." He was being stalwart, but his voice was thick with emotion.

"You're pale as a ghost." The EMT who had given me the blanket came around the back of the ambulance. "Let's get you flat and elevate your feet." She tipped me onto the gurney and put a wedge under my legs. I hadn't been aware of being dizzy, but once I was on my back I felt better. I didn't understand why I was so affected by finding Andie's body. I'd found dead bodies before and it hadn't been this much of a blow since the first one. Toward the end of my career in New York in investment banking I'd suffered from panic attacks. The stress and the travel had piled up on me. But since I'd returned to Busman's Harbor the attacks had tapered to nothing. It had been at least two years since I'd suffered one.

"Do you know when I can go?" I asked the EMT.

"I'll speak to the sergeant."

It felt like ages, but Sergeant Dundee finally told me I could go home. He said to expect a call from the state police Major Crimes Unit to come in and give a formal statement.

"Do you know who's coming from Major Crimes?"

"Lieutenant Jerry Binder and Sergeant Thomas Flynn."

I exhaled with relief. "I know them."

"I've heard."

A police car took me to the bottom of the private road that led to the farm. My car had to stay awhile longer, something about tire tracks, which didn't bother me. I didn't feel up to driving, anyway.

Chris was waiting in his pickup truck when I arrived. He jumped from the cab and came over to hug me when I got out of the patrol car. "Are you okay?"

"I'm not."

He stepped back to look at me. "Were you hurt?"

"The EMT was worried about shock."

"Let's get you home." He put his arm around me and helped me to his truck. He lifted me up to the seat and then closed the door gently.

Later that afternoon, Chris drove me back to Damariscotta to pick up my car and have my interview at the request of Lieutenant Binder and Sergeant Flynn of the state police Major Crimes Unit.

Chris had been lovely and solicitous all day. I was keenly aware that time was ticking down to the start of the season. If he didn't have his homeowners' lawns and gardens perfectly turned out by Memorial Day, he would hear about it, maybe even lose some customers. And though he kept up a cheerful and distracting conversation, Andie had been his friend, not mine, and he needed room to mourn, too. Room he would have had if I hadn't been the one to find her body.

The police had moved my car to the lot at the town office building. Very convenient.

"Are you sure you don't want me to stay?" Chris asked. Despite my protests, he had walked me to the door.

"I'm fine. You go," I assured him.

The Damariscotta police force was even smaller than Busman's Harbor's—four sworn officers including the chief. They'd add some part-timers during the tourist season, but before Memorial Day they weren't yet on the job. The civilian receptionist, a middle-aged woman with tightly curled brown hair and look of permanent disdain, took my name and told me Binder and Flynn would be with me as soon as they finished another interview.

I'd waited about ten minutes when a large oak door opened. Tom Flynn ushered Andie's employee Josh, who looked pale and shaky, into the hallway. It had been months since I'd seen Flynn. He hadn't changed a bit— same military bearing, same board-flat stomach enhanced by a well-cut brown suit.

Flynn handed the poor kid a card and said, "Let us

know if you remember anything else." Then he spotted me, "Julia, come on in."

He took me by the arm and guided me into the room he and Binder had commandeered for their incident room. The town offices were in a former school. I couldn't tell if the space we were in had been a classroom or an office, but its proportions were designed to make children feel small and powerless, and it made me feel small and powerless, too. Jerry Binder rose from behind a big oak teachers' desk and came forward to give me a hug. This wasn't the way they treated most of their witnesses, but the three of us were so far beyond that it didn't matter.

When we were seated, we caught up a little. Binder had a ski-slope nose and a bald head and had recently taken to wearing reading glasses, a situation that aggravated him to no end. He reported that his wife, also a member of the state police, was doing fine. Their two boys were growing like weeds. Under intense questioning by me, Flynn stated he was still single, a state of affairs that never failed to surprise me. Like the ex-soldier he was, he stood up straight and sat up straight. Even the short brown hairs on his head stood at attention. As always, he looked as though he took all the time and energy that would have been spent with a romantic partner and used it at the gym.

The pleasantries over, Binder looked at his laptop monitor and Flynn pulled his notebook, which was open on the desk, toward him. They both sat on the same side. I was on the other. "We'd better get started," Binder said. "Lots to do today. Let's begin at the beginning. Why did you go to the Great River Oyster Farm this morning?"

"Andie Greatorex asked me to come over. I'm sure you've already heard she received a ransom note last night."

"For her stolen oyster eggs," Binder said.

"Seed, or spat. Stolen oyster seed." I hadn't meant to sound pedantic with my newfound oyster knowledge. But I didn't want them to go around town calling them eggs. It wouldn't help.

"Why did Ms. Greatorex ask for your opinion about the ransom note? Were you friends?"

"She was more a friend of Chris's." Beside me, I felt Flynn's stiff posture stiffen further. He and Binder hadn't started out as fans of Chris's. Chris hadn't much liked them either, especially after they arrested him for a murder he didn't commit. It was all pretty much water under the bridge by this point, but Binder and Flynn still trod carefully where Chris was concerned. "I liked Andie," I said. "I wish I had gotten to know her better. She wanted to talk to me about the note because I'd been helping her figure out who stole the seed."

"And she approached you to help because . . ." Flynn paused pregnantly. I shrugged and smiled. "Never mind," he conceded. "I get it."

"The local PD think the ransom note was a hoax," Binder told me.

"I figured that was why they arrived at Andie's with their sirens and lights on last night. Is that what you think?"

Binder took off the hated reading glasses and looked directly at me. "We agree it looks amateurish in the extreme. It's handwritten, doesn't warn against involving the police, includes no proof the sender actually has the, er, seed, and asks for payment to be left in a place that is easily watched." *Exactly what I had thought.* Binder continued. "Then again, the robbery wasn't the height of sophistication, either. Knock the victim down, kick her, grab the pails and run." He leaned both elbows on the big oak desk. "The truth is, I've never dealt with a ransom demand. I've worked on kidnappings resulting from custody fights, and abductions related to sex crimes. Neither involve ransom." He flashed a grin but then quickly rearranged his features to match the seriousness of the task at hand. "I guarantee I have never, ever worked on a kidnapping where there were tens of thousands of victims."

"I thought the note was a hoax, too," I said. "But now—"

"Now that Ms. Greatorex is dead, you're having second thoughts."

"Not about the ransom note per se, but about the whole series of events." I described the petty harassments, and then the robbery. They'd heard pretty much everything about the assault and theft of the seed from the local police, including the description of the suspect Andie had given. They hadn't heard about the nuisance incidents.

"I assume the Damariscotta police followed up on the obvious suspects for the robbery, the employees at the hatchery who knew what time Andie would be picking up the seed."

"They did. We'll do it all again now that the robbery is related to a murder, but we've looked at their statements and I'm not expecting to find anything."

"If the robbery and the delivery of the ransom note are related, we're talking about someone who is watching Andie's cottage and farm."

"Maybe," Flynn said, which in his case passed for enthusiastic agreement.

"What did you think of Ms. Greatorex?" Binder asked.

"We'd just met. You've already talked to people who knew her much better than I did." I looked at the door Josh had exited through.

"We're interested in your perspective." They honestly seemed to be. Binder looked away from his monitor. Flynn looked up from his notebook.

"I admired her. I thought she was level-headed. Brave. She built a great business. Yesterday we spent the whole morning together while she showed me around the farm." My voice got quavery at the end. *Had it only been yesterday?*

After that, Binder took me painstaking through the events of the morning while Flynn took notes, occasionally asking a clarifying question. I was exhausted at the end of it. The morning wasn't as traumatic relived as lived, but it was still a terrible experience.

When we were done, Flynn opened his mouth as if to follow up. Out of the corner of my eye, I caught Binder giving a slight shake of his head and he typed busily into his laptop. He was giving me a minute to pull myself together and I appreciated it.

Finally, Binder said, "Did Ms. Greatorex give you any idea who she suspected?"

"She had applied to lease more area on the river to expand her operation. A public hearing was scheduled for tomorrow. She had significant opposition. She didn't give me specific names of people who objected to the lease. It was as if she couldn't bring herself believe any of her friends or fellow citizens could assault and rob her. I found some names on my own and had talked to several people yesterday."

Flynn raised his eyebrows at me, hand hovering over his notepad, so I continued.

"I talked to Mack Owen, who used to be Andie's business partner. And to Ken Farrow, another oyster farmer. His is a smaller farm, not established as a business yet. He's concerned Andie's new lease would keep him from being able to expand. Bob Campbell is kind of the go-to lobsterman on the river. The lobstermen object to the amount of the river that's currently leased. They're unhappy they're losing bottom for their traps. Pinney Kirwin is a neighbor who doesn't want any farms on the river. She thinks it should be preserved for the enjoyment of the abutters and for recreational boating. She saw Andie's lease expansion as something of a last stand."

"The local police put us on to Mack Owen. We gather he was a romantic partner as well as a business partner. He's coming in for an interview right after you, for background on Ms. Greatorex at this point. But thank you for the rest of these names. Did you draw any conclusions?"

I shook my head. "It was way too early. None of them match the physical description of the assailant. Which brings me to two other people." I described the confrontation between Andie and Lacey Brenneman and how Lacey's dinner companion was the same physical type as the robber. "I took photos of him. I'll text them to you. But Lacey and her boyfriend couldn't have delivered the ransom note. I saw them in Crowley's in Busman's Harbor when that happened."

Binder wound up the interview. "Julia, thanks so much

for this. We'll be in touch if we need you. If you remember anything else or have other thoughts, you know how to find us." He stood and so did Flynn.

I got to my feet as well. "One other thing you should know. Bob Campbell is my uncle."

Flynn laughed.

"Of course he is." Binder smiled. "It's Maine."

CHAPTER SEVEN

I woke up to the smell of bacon and coffee same as I did almost every day of the year. A low murmur of conversation punctuated by the scrape of a metal spatula on a hot grill floated up the stairs to my apartment.

"Pancakes?" Chris asked, opening a sleepy eye.

"Pancakes," I said.

Downstairs, Gus's restaurant was filled with the usual crowd, the lobstermen and the people who worked in the shops, B & Bs, and tour boats. You could feel the energy revving up to Memorial Day and the beginning of the season. The days of lingering over a second cup of coffee were behind us. The tables turned over quickly with people shuttling up and down the stairs to the street-side front door.

I was surprised to see Lieutenant Binder and Sergeant Flynn in a booth. They were both fans of Gus's and they'd been around enough, often in the company of the local Busman's Harbor cops, that Gus was willing to serve them. Strangely, for a restaurant owner in a resort town that made its money on tourists, Gus's restaurant welcomed only people he knew or people who came in with someone he knew. I used to think this policy was insane, and it was certainly illegal, but now that I'd been back in town for a few years, I got it. We all needed a place where we could be offstage and comfortable, especially at the height of the tourist season.

Binder and Flynn had obviously recently arrived. They didn't have food or even drinks in front of them. Binder waved us over to join them.

Chris greeted the cops and sat down in the booth. I went behind the counter and retrieved a full coffee carafe and three mugs. Because we lived upstairs and ran a dinner restaurant in his space during the off-season, Gus tolerated behavior from us he'd never put up with from others. I took the mugs back to our booth and poured the coffee, refilling other people's cups as I returned. So as not to raise Gus's wrath, I started a new pot before filling a glass with tepid water for Flynn. Gus was at the grill with his back to me. "Be with you in a minute," he grumbled. "Unless you'd like to cook your own breakfast."

I skedaddled back to the booth and handed Flynn his water.

"Thanks."

"What brings you to Busman's Harbor?" I asked. We were forty minutes from their crime scene.

"Interview," Flynn answered.

I suspected the interview had been timed to facilitate their breakfast at Gus's. I wondered if it was with Andie's angry ex-employee, Lacey Brenneman, who, given her presence at Crowley's the other night, might live here in town. Maybe Binder and Flynn planned to interview her boyfriend, too. I hoped they did. It would mean they were taking my information seriously.

Gus showed up, order pad in hand. Like always, he plucked the stub of a pencil from where it had been hidden behind his ear by his abundant white hair. "What'll it be?"

I ordered blueberry pancakes, as did Chris. The Maine blueberries would be frozen at that time of year, but it hardly mattered. Binder went for Gus's renowned clam hash with eggs over easy and home fries. Flynn ordered two soft-boiled eggs.

"What kind of toast?" Gus asked in a well-practiced ritual.

"No toast." Flynn also knew his lines.

"Wheat it is." Gus twirled on his heels, a neat move for a man so old no one in town knew his age except his wife. He headed back to the kitchen area behind the counter.

"We understand you were a friend of Ms. Greatorex," Binder said to Chris. "We're sorry for your loss."

"Thank you." Chris acknowledged the words with a dip of his head.

"And you are also a friend of Mack Owen. What do you think of him?" Flynn asked.

I had wondered if Binder and Flynn would talk about the case in front of Chris, but apparently I had it wrong. They wanted to talk *to* Chris.

"Mack's a great guy." Chris answered without hesitation.

"We spoke to him yesterday," Binder said.

"I heard that was the plan." I'd given Chris a pretty detailed download on my interview the evening before.

"He was a business partner and a romantic partner of the deceased." Flynn let the statement hang in the air.

"A long time ago," Chris said. "Years."

"Five years," Binder confirmed. "More than enough time to change her will and life insurance beneficiary. Yet she didn't. Everything goes to Owen. Seems like a glaring oversight."

Chris's eyebrows rose. He clearly hadn't known that. He took a sip of coffee. "Maybe not," he finally responded. "Andie didn't have family. The farm was her baby. She'd want it to go to someone who could take care of it. Mack is the obvious person. Plus they were still close friends."

"There wasn't any hostility between them after the break-up?" Binder asked.

"None." Chris said it in a way that didn't encourage more questions. The monosyllabic response made me wonder if Chris was telling us everything. I was sure Binder and Flynn were equally doubtful. Though both Andie and Mack separately had said the same thing. Somehow their friendship had survived their breakup.

Gus showed up with the food, including two slices of wheat toast dripping in butter to go with Flynn's eggs. The arrival of our meal effectively ended our conversation about the case. As I dug into my blueberry pancakes, smothered with real Maine maple syrup, we talked about the weather, the Red Sox, and the prospects for the coming tourist season, all mandatory Maine subjects.

Gus handed us each a bill. He didn't take checks, credit cards or payment apps, which played havoc with

Binder and Flynn's expense reports, and yet they still came. Binder put cash on the table. The detectives excused themselves got up, leaving Chris and me.

"They've got Mack in their sights," Chris said.

"He's the ex. And he inherits it all. That doesn't help. But I'm sure they're looking at other suspects. Why else would they be in Busman's Harbor doing interviews?"

Chris shrugged. "Maybe. But I don't feel good about this."

By the time we said good-bye and I headed to my office, I wasn't feeling so good, either. I wasn't worried about Binder and Flynn railroading Mack Owen. I trusted them more than that. I was feeling down and sad about Andie.

When I reached my mother's house, I didn't go inside, though there was Snowden Family Clambake work to be done. A force I couldn't name drew me not to my office but to my car. I headed for Damariscotta and Andie's farm.

I was surprised there was no sign of police presence at the bottom of the private road into Great River Farm. I drove in and parked in front of the shop. Josh was inside, so I opened the door to let him know I was on the property. I didn't want to scare the poor kid. He'd been through enough the day before.

Despite my best intentions, when the door opened, and the little bell rang, he took three giant steps backward. "I came to work because I didn't know what else to do. It's early in the season. There may not be any customers, but I felt like I should be here in case people came by." He stuttered out the explanation, as if he were the one who had to justify being on Andie's property, not me. "I figure the new boss would want to sell this stuff, whoever it is."

I scanned the shelves full of merchandise—the oyster plates, the Great River T-shirts, the gloves, the knives. The knives. In the plastic bin with the other oyster knives were several with the same blue handles as the one I had most recently seen protruding from the neck of Andie Greatorex's corpse. The image made me shiver. I reached up, hesitantly, and picked one out of the bin. It said MACK'S OYSTER SHACK along with the restaurant's oyster shell logo. I touched my fingertip to the point and recoiled. As Mack had shown me, it was deadly sharp. "You sell oyster knives from Mack's Shack," I said.

"It's a kind of a cross promotion thing they do. Did." Josh corrected himself. "Andie sends people along to Mack's for a meal. He sends people over here to see how the oysters are farmed." His nervous habit of flicking his head or using his hands to get his bangs out of his eyes was working overtime.

It was interesting that the knives were right on the property. "Yesterday morning, did Andie seem different to you, worried or scared?" I asked him.

Josh shook his head from side to side in staccato bursts. "No. Like I told the cops yesterday, everything was normal, like any other day."

But how could it have been? She'd received the ransom note the night before. Someone had robbed her, and now someone was likely watching her house. Andie behaved like it was like any other day. I would have been freaked out.

"If she'd said she was scared, I would have told her not to go," Josh said. "Or I would have gone with her and sat in the boat while she dove. I wish I had."

The poor kid. "It's not your fault. Whatever happened to Andie, you didn't make it happen and you probably couldn't have stopped it."

"Thanks," he said.

"I'm going to head down to the dock for a minute to look around."

If he thought that was strange, Josh didn't say so. He busied himself filling shelves with stock for a season that might never come. I understood the impulse. Sometimes it was necessary to believe in stability in the face of sudden and tragic change.

I walked toward the dock, feeling the pull of the steep hill in my calves. Somewhere, someone was working on a house or boat. The whack, whack, whack of a hammer hitting wood carried across the water. The river came into view through the leaves. A sailboat cut through the current. When I came around the bend at the bottom, a boat was tied up at the dock. Not at the end, where Andie's body had been, but on the side. At first, I thought it was Andie's, that the police had found it and brought it back, but this boat was considerably smaller and had an outboard motor. When I reached the dock, a pair of legs was bent over one of the upwellers, the person's back and head invisible to me. It was too late to retreat. "Hey!" I called out, not wanting to surprise him.

Ken Farrow straightened up so quickly he nearly lost his balance. "You scared me."

"It's a little creepy being here," I admitted. "What are you doing?"

"I came over to take care of Andie's upwellers. I figured no one was doing it and I didn't want whoever the heir is to lose the entire new crop." He paused; his mouth set in a grim line. "As I told you, Andie had promised to sell some of these babies to me. You could say I'm protecting my investment." He looked toward the end of the dock. "A heck of a thing. I heard you found her."

"I did."

"From the moment the cops and paramedics arrived, I watched it all through a pair of binoculars from the end of my dock. I don't know when the last of them left. It was after dark. It must have been terrible for you." His voice softened in sympathy.

"It was. I think that's why I came back today. I needed to see the river and farm again, at peace as they should be, not with all the vehicles and first responders . . ." My voice trailed off.

"You must have been interviewed by the police," Farrow said. "Do they have any idea . . . ?"

"Nothing they shared." The news that Mack Owen was Andie's heir was not mine to broadcast. "This means the end of Andie's lease application," I said. "You must be relieved."

He grunted. "I'm not relieved it happened this way. I admired Andie. All the oyster farmers did. She and Mack started with next to nothing and made a success of this place. She was good for the local economy, good to the land, good to the river, and supplied tens of thousands of people with a wonderful eating experience. I'll not say anything bad about her." He gestured toward the upwellers. "If you don't mind, I'll get on with it."

"Of course. I'm going to wander a little. I'll stay out of your way."

After I left Farrow, I entered the sorting shed. It looked exactly as it had the day before. I thought about walking to the end of the dock where I'd found Andie. I might have if I'd been alone, but it seemed too morbid and weird with Farrow there. The hammering I'd heard on the way down to the water had continued. I said good-bye to Farrow and headed in the direction of the noise.

The river echoes sound so I wasn't sure where the hammering was coming from, but as I moved through the trees toward Pinney Kirwin's house it got louder, and I felt like I was on the right track.

Sure enough, as the trees opened onto the big lawn, I saw a figure in the distance high on a ladder replacing the shingle siding on a third-floor turret. I hurried up the lawn.

Was he? Could he be? Even from my weird angle, he looked like Andie's ex-employee's boyfriend. He was dressed all in black, black jeans, long-sleeved T-shirt, and shoes. He had the same scruffy, longish hair. He was too far up the ladder for me to see his features one hundred percent clearly. I stepped back and observed him on the ladder. Same rangy body, just like the one Andie had described for her assailant.

"Lookout below!" An old, weathered shingle fell into the small pile below the ladder. I looked up to see the young guy smiling at me. He didn't look particularly safe up there. Nor did it look like a one-person job.

"Hi!" he called. "Looking for someone?"

"Is Ms. Kirwin here?"

"Don't think so."

"Were you up there working yesterday morning?" I asked.

He had pulled a fresh shingle out of the satchel to replace the one that had landed beside me, but he paused before hammering to answer me. "You mean when the body was found over there? No. I wasn't up here. I wasn't even on the property. Missed all the excitement." He gave a little laugh.

He wasn't being insensitive. He didn't know I'd found Andie's body, but I bristled, nonetheless. He got back to banging and I looked carefully at the house. The side I was on now, the river side, was in much rougher shape than side by the driveway I'd entered from two days before. There were dozens of split and failing shingles, maybe hundreds. And the fascia board and wooden gutters were coming away in places.

Having a house on the water meant constant work. I knew that from my mother's experience and from keeping our dining pavilion and outbuildings spiffed up for the clambakes. Not to mention the ongoing renovations of Windsholme, the abandoned mansion on Morrow Island, the private island my mother owned where we ran the clambakes.

Lots of people adhered to the view that you should paint one side of your house every year, starting over when you got around again, like the Golden Gate Bridge. The river side of Pinney Kirwin's house looked like it suffered from years of neglect.

The next time the guy stopped hammering I called up to him. "I'm Julia Snowden, by the way."

"Clark," he called back. *Only one name. Was it his first or last?*

"Have the police talked to you about Andie Greatorex's murder?"

He shook the shaggy curls. "No. Why would they? I wasn't here."

"Do you know if the police talked to Ms. Kirwin?"

"Nope." One-name-Clark went back to hammering.

I turned back to the river, trying to think of a way to ask if he knew Lacey. Out of the corner of my eye I saw Pinney in a boat on the river, rowing energetically toward her dock. Her oars cut the water in powerful, even sweeps. The boat moved steadily and swiftly. Though she faced the other way, she angled directly toward her dock in well-practiced movements. I went to meet her.

After Pinney tied up the rowboat, she removed the oars from the oarlocks and piled them on the dock. I reached out to help her as she stepped out of the rocking boat. She held on briefly and I felt the strength her forearm. Then she dropped my hand like it was on fire and moved on.

"No need," she said. She took off the ancient orange life-preserver she wore over a Kelly-green sweatshirt and left it on top of the oars. "I row to Dodge Cove and back every day, May to October, rain or shine. It's important to stay active." Beneath her denim culottes, her legs were tanned, which I hadn't noticed before. Her feet were in pink tennis shoes with white Peds peeking over the top. Her hair, held in place by another color-coordinated headband, looked like she hadn't been out on the water at all.

Dodge Cove was a good three miles away and the trip would have been done against the current for half of it. I was impressed, but I wasn't surprised. These summer women, these paragons, often had unwavering views about keeping fit. Whatever they did, be it vicious games of tennis, distance swimming in the cold Atlantic Ocean, or powerwalking through the center of town, scattering hapless day-trippers in their wake, they did it rain or shine, unless the weatherman absolutely forbade it.

"Did you drive?" Pinney asked. "I didn't see a car when I came around the river bend."

"I walked over from next door."

I followed her up the lawn. When we were within forty feet of the house, she shaded her eyes and called up to Clark. "Is that all you've got done? What have you been doing all morning?"

"It's my fault," I said. "I distracted him." I had, though only for a moment. I hoped defending Clark now might earn me points I could use with him later.

"Harrumph." She dropped the hand and looked at me. "Let Clark get on about his business. He has a lot to finish up and if he doesn't finish it today, who knows when he'll be able to spare me a minute again."

From the way she spoke it, I understood Clark to be his first name.

Up on the ladder, Clark laughed. "Good help is hard to find."

"Indeed." Pinney looked from him to me and then stared pointedly at the woods along the property line and Andie's farm beyond. I understood I'd been dismissed. Being Jacqueline Snowden's daughter had cut some ice when I pulled up in her driveway and knocked politely on her door, but it didn't help me when I'd entered her property stealthily and engaged with the help.

I turned and walked back across the big lawn.

CHAPTER EIGHT

Ken Farrow and his boat were gone when I got back to Andie's property. I stopped to tell Josh I was leaving, but the shop was dark inside, and a CLOSED sign hung on the door. I got into my Subaru and headed for Mack's Oyster Shack. Everyone has to eat, right?

The parking lot was half-full and the restaurant moderately busy when I got inside. The hostess walked me to the raw bar where I hoped I'd run into Mack. Instead, the cheerful blonde bartender came over from the big, square bar and took my order for iced tea and told me she'd be right back with it.

While she was gone, I checked my phone to make sure all was well with the clambake. A text from my brother-in-law Sonny asked if I'd gotten around to screening the applicants to work at the clam fire yet and reminded me he would be the last word on any hires. **Yes, got it!** I texted back. I added the exclamation mark to appear cheerful and chipper, though I feared it made me sound as annoyed as I was. I was annoyed because he was right. I needed to be back at my desk filling out the clambake crew, which I positively, definitely would be after lunch.

After firing off the text I sat and looked around. There was a glass jar filled with oyster knives on the bar. They had the same blue handle and white print for the name and logo as the ones I had so recently seen at Andie's shop, and before that sticking out of Andie's neck. The jar was in a handy place for whoever was working behind the raw bar, but any reasonably long-armed customer could also reach it if he or she really wanted a knife. As an experiment I tried it, easily plucking a knife from the jar. I noticed the Great River oysters had vanished from the raw bar display; the sign that had marked them had been removed. There would be no Great Rivers for a while.

The bartender returned with my drink. I was about to order some oysters when Mack entered the restaurant. His shoulders were slumped which emphasized his slight frame and he seemed to drag himself across the room, so different than the man so full of energy and enthusiasm I'd met only two days before. He stopped and chatted with the hostess and then started toward a door off the restaurant floor marked OFFICE. But he stopped when he spotted me at the raw bar and came in my direction.

"Julia," he said when he reached me. "Just who I wanted to see. Do you have a minute?"

"Sure."

"Can you bring two lunch specials to my office?" he asked the bartender. He turned to me. "Our Friday fish sandwich and fries. Is that okay?"

"Absolutely."

"Come on back." I followed him to his office. Job applications crowded his desktop just as they crowded mine. He sat behind his desk and I took the guest chair right in front of it. The room was tiny. In restaurants, square footage didn't get wasted on sumptuous offices, even for the owner.

"I've come from the police station. Second interview," Mack said. "I guess that makes sense. I was Andie's business partner and her boyfriend for over ten years. She doesn't have any family so I'm the person closest to her. But the police think it's more than that." He looked at me. "You found her. What do you know?"

I gave him a barebones description of my morning the day before. I didn't linger on the description of Andie's body. They'd been close.

When I was done, Mack closed his eyes and kept them closed for what felt like a long time. "Why do they keep asking questions about my oyster knives?" he finally asked.

"What kind of questions?"

"Where do we get them? How many do we have? Who has access to them? The answers are we have tons of them, and anyone who wants to can walk off with one and lots of people do. They're our most frequently stolen item."

"I get it." At the clambake we set the tables with nutcrackers to use on lobster claws. Those nutcrackers walked off the island in ridiculous numbers. We'd tried selling them in the gift shop as a hint they should be paid for. I had the JOATS, the Jacks-Of-All-Trades who bussed the tables, collect them as soon as the main meal was over. Nothing worked. I'd been tempted to frisk people as they got on the boat back to the mainland, but I didn't think that would go over well.

I wasn't going to disclose to Mack things Binder and Flynn had told me in confidence, but I also wasn't going to lie about things I'd seen with my own eyes. "Andie had a knife with a blue handle sticking out of her neck when I found her. I think it was one of yours."

The color drained from his face. "They think I killed her."

"My advice is not to talk to the police again without a lawyer present. I strongly recommend Cuthie Cuthbertson. He helped Chris when he got accused of murder three years ago." Cuthie was a roly-poly man with pomaded hair who wore his suits so large the trousers pooled around his shoes and the jacket sleeves covered his hands. At a glance, he didn't inspire confidence, but he was a brilliant defense attorney. The best in the county.

The bartender arrived with two plates. Each held an enormous piece of fried fish on a toasted roll, French fries, and little cups of coleslaw, tartar sauce and ketchup. She opened her mouth as if about to ask if we needed anything else, but then looked at her boss's face and left the room as quickly as she could.

I was starving and took a bite. The sandwich was delicious, crispy on the outside, well-cooked, light, white fish on the inside. Frying seafood is a skill unto itself, and Mack's Shack had it down.

Mack looked at his plate and pushed it away, like he might never feel like eating again. "You and Chris were here asking about Andie's robbery and the next day she was dead. Chris told me you were investigating for Andie. The robbery and her murder must be connected. Did you get anywhere before Andie was killed?"

"Not really." I returned my sandwich to my plate on the edge of Mack's desk.

"Did you talk to Bob Campbell, like I told you?"

"I did. The lobstermen don't like the idea of more of the river being leased. But he denied absolutely he or anyone he knew had ever done anything to Andie."

"That's rich. There was a table full of them in here on locals' night bragging about interfering with the oyster farmers' cages and stealing their buoys. You need to make sure the police know that. If I tell the police, they'll assume I'm trying to get them off my back, but you can tell them."

"I didn't witness the harassments and Andie didn't accuse anyone when I asked her. I'm not going to pass rumors along to the cops." It was time to be honest. "You should know Bob Campbell is my uncle. He's married to my late father's sister. I was in and out of their house the whole time I was growing up."

"Your uncle was trying to throw you off the scent." Mack made it a statement, not a question. "Julia, will you help me?"

"Help you how?"

"Help me convince the police I didn't do anything to Andie. None of it." His voice grew thick. "I loved her. Not romantically, not anymore, but as a friend. I would never do anything to hurt Andie."

"What do you think I can do?"

"Chris is always bragging about what a great investigator you are. You've helped the state cops plenty of times. These guys know you. They'll listen to you. Who am I to them? A suspect."

I'd thought this might have been why he wanted to meet privately. Nonetheless, I was taken aback. He was a suspect, probably Binder and Flynn's prime suspect. I gave him the same caveats I'd given Andie.

"I've helped Lieutenant Binder and Sergeant Flynn by providing local information about Busman's Harbor. I'm not sure how I can help in this situation."

"You're already in this situation," Mack pointed out. "You're in it up to your neck."

He wasn't wrong. "I'll do what I can. I'll think about who else might be involved. But I won't lie, and I won't withhold what I find from the police."

He waved his hands. "Of course not. I would never ask you to lie. Or withhold. Whatever you find out is only going to help me anyway."

I had finished my sandwich while we'd talked and felt like I needed to get moving. I stood and thanked him for lunch. "I'll do my best. No guarantees."

"No guarantees," he repeated. "One more thing. We're having a time for Andie, here, tomorrow, at five-thirty. She doesn't have anybody. I want to do something before the season starts to give folks a chance to pay their respects."

A "time" in New England meant a gathering celebrating someone or something. It might mark a birthday, a retirement, a political victory, or a passing. The honored person might be living or dead.

"Okay," I said. "Tomorrow. Five-thirty. I'll tell Chris."

My aunt's car wasn't in the driveway. She was undoubtedly at work. My uncle's truck was there, but *My Sharona* wasn't at her dock.

I knocked and yoo-hooed at the front door with no results. I was on my way back to my car when I turned and saw Uncle Bob maneuver *My Sharona* to the dock and tie her up.

She was a good-looking boat, sturdy and well-cared for. Empty lobster traps were piled in her stern. It was early in the season and most likely he'd been out alone, dropping traps in his favorite places. He wouldn't hire on an assistant, called a sternman regardless of gender, until closer to the summer.

Uncle Bob unplugged three pieces of equipment from the boat's console, the depth finder, GPS, and radio and carried them toward his shed. When he got to the shed, he put them on the ground and unlocked the padlock. He was a little deaf and between the wind and the water, he didn't hear me until I was less than twenty feet from him. By that point he was inside the shed stowing his gear.

He came out of the shed, looked around and then slammed its flimsy wooden door shut. "Julia, you nearly scared me to death."

"I called. You didn't hear me."

He snapped the padlock shut. "What brings you here twice in a week? As if I couldn't guess. Andie Greatorex."

I admitted that was true. I was glad my aunt wasn't around. Uncle Bob might be more honest in her absence.

Uncle Bob started toward the house. "I got to get cleaned up. C'mon."

I waited at the kitchen table until he appeared at the top of the stairs in jeans and a flannel shirt. His salt-and-pepper hair was damp. He filled the percolator with ground coffee and water and then sat across from me. "What do you want to know?"

I cleared my throat. He was my senior, a cherished relative who had been nothing but good to me. "Andie told me she was being harassed. Nothing serious, no loss of her crop, but buoys and cages tampered with."

"So you mentioned." He drummed the fingers of his left hand on the tabletop, staring at me.

"You and your buddies have been overheard in public places bragging about interfering with the oyster farmers' gear."

Uncle Bob finally blinked. "It's no secret we don't love it that so much of the brackish river water is leased. But I'd say there's a lot more talk than action. When the boys say they did this or that, they're always exaggerating."

"Yet Andie's gear actually was interfered with. And now she's dead."

The color drained from his face. "You can't believe I had anything to do with that."

My face was suddenly hot, as if the blood gone from his face had flooded mine. "No."

"Who's telling these tales anyway?" he demanded.

I wasn't going to give Mack up. "I heard it around. You and your pals haven't been discreet. The opposite in fact."

He grunted, then stood and poured us each a mug of coffee. Until two days before, I hadn't been in his house for seven years, but I was still so comfortable there I could open the refrigerator and fetch the milk for both of us. He nodded when his coffee had turned a rich tan color and I put the milk away.

"No lobsterman did this to Andie." He said it authoritatively.

"How can you be so sure?"

"Because I know them. And because, though we com-

plain about the farmers the reality is we respect them. I'd
rather deal with a hundred oyster farmers than one hedge
fund manager jerk on a million-dollar sailboat. The farmers have a different way of life, but like us they work on
the water and they see themselves as stewards of the environment. And if the politicians and bureaucrats in Augusta lease too much of the river, that's on them and their
greed, not the oyster farmers. We gave Andie a hard time,
but to a man, we liked her and respected her."

His eyes were wet, his voice choked with emotion
when he finished speaking. Andie had been part of the
fabric of his life on the river. Her passing affected him,
too.

I waited for him to compose himself. "Do you have
thoughts about who could have done this? Have you
heard anything?"

"Nothing." His voice was back to normal. Mainers
buried their emotions deep.

"You sent me to Ken Farrow when I first came
around."

He lifted the mug and swallowed a gulp of the coffee.
I did the same. For all the fancy coffee shops I'd been in
when I traveled for work, there was no better cup of coffee than the one that came out of the old-fashioned percolator in my aunt and uncle's kitchen.

"I mentioned Farrow because when you came around
before because you were asking about the robbery,"
Uncle Bob said. "I thought, who would benefit? Only
someone who could take care of the oyster seed. Ken was
opposed to Andie's lease expansion. But he wouldn't kill
her. I can't imagine." He shook his head. "I can't imagine
anyone I know killing Andie."

"It turns out Ken doesn't have any upwellers." I thought I'd nip the rumors about Farrow in the bud. "He was buying oysters large enough to put in his cages from Andie."

Uncle Bob's brow creased over his nose. "Makes sense. It takes at least three years to get a crop to market. Buying from Andie would speed that up. I didn't know."

The talk turned to other things. Uncle Bob needed a new sternman for the summer season and asked if I knew anyone. "I wish," I said. "I'm trying to fill my own positions. If I hear of anyone, I'll let you know."

We hugged good-bye at the front door, and I climbed into the Subaru. He stood on his front steps waving until I couldn't see him anymore.

CHAPTER NINE

I swung by the town offices hoping to catch Binder and Flynn in and available. It was a long shot, but I was eager to tell them I'd seen the surnameless Clark working on Pinney Kirwin's house. He was connected to two people who had problems with Andie—Lacey Brenneman, the angry ex-employee, and Pinney Kirwin, the angry neighbor. He met the physical description of the robber who'd knocked Andie down and stolen the seed. He had to figure in the case.

Binder's unmarked car wasn't in the parking lot and when I went inside, the civilian receptionist informed me they'd left for Augusta. "Autopsy," she said, and then grimaced. Murder wasn't the usual thing around her office.

I had both Binder and Flynn's cell numbers in my phone. I got back in the Subaru and called each and left a message to call me. Then I hit the road to Busman's Harbor.

When I pulled into my mother's driveway, I groaned. My brother-in-law Sonny was hard at work putting the screens up on Mom's front porch. It was an annual ritual. The screens were wooden, heavy to carry from the garage and warped so that fitting them into the frames and tightening the fasteners always resulted in a lot of salty language, no matter who did the chore. Sonny Ramsey had been married to my younger sister for a dozen years, since she'd graduated from high school already pregnant with my niece Page. The tinges of drama and tragedy that had accompanied those events were long past. Page was an eleven-year-old delight. Her toddler brother, my nephew Jack, kept us laughing. Sonny and my sister Livvie were, against all odds, still married. I couldn't understand it, but they were crazy about each other.

Since I'd come back to run the clambake, Sonny and I had to find our own relationship. I had, for all intents and purposes, replaced him as the boss. He'd done his best to run the clambake after my Dad died, but the brutally short tourist season and the razor thin margins of a food business had required a firmer hand on the tiller than he was willing or able to provide. We'd eventually found our way and retreated to our respective corners, me in charge of the business end and he as the Bakemaster, in charge of the clambake fire.

Sonny waved as I pulled past him in the driveway and around to the back of the house to the three-car garage. He made it upstairs to the clambake office before I did. I flinched involuntarily when I saw the employment applications spread out on my desk.

"Have you got people for me to interview, Julia? You know we open in a week, right? And I've got no one working with me at the clambake fire."

I knew it all right. One of Sonny's regular employees, a schoolteacher from Maryland, had married and announced he wouldn't be spending his summers with us anymore. The other longtime employee had died. And my attempt to hire Chris's brother at the end of the previous season had been a disaster. As things stood now, Sonny would be working alone. Which was impossible. If worse came to worst, I could beg Chris to help him. He'd filled in from time to time in the past. But I hated to do it. And it was a Band-Aid at best. Chris had three jobs in the summer as it was.

"I'll find at least two interviews for you by the end of today," I said. "We'll schedule them for as soon as possible. Tomorrow." It was a rash promise. Working at the fire required strength, agility, fearlessness, and maturity. Was there anyone like that in the pile of applications? Were there *two* such people?

Sonny crossed his big arms over his barrel chest. His buzz cut was showing less and less red hair and more and more scalp. "See you do. I got to get back to the screens."

"Mom appreciates it!" I called after him.

I dug into the pile. Most of the applications were simple, handwritten forms prospective employees picked up at our ticket kiosk and completed with a pen. A few came from inquiries about jobs I received over email, from friends of friends of our college and teacher employees, who had recommended us. Those were usually filled out using a word-processing program, but the bulk were handwritten.

I quickly sorted the applications into piles. The high

school students to consider as JOATs, our entry level position. Some applications went into the pile for potential waitstaff. I knew I wouldn't be able to fill every slot with someone with experience, but in addition to the meager number of applicants who had worked as servers, I added former bussers and hosts, anyone with restaurant experience. Basically, there was only one meal at the clambake— clam chowder, followed by twin lobsters, soft-shell clams called steamers, a potato, onion, ear of corn and a hard-boiled egg, followed by blueberry grunt with vanilla ice cream. We substituted chicken for the few guests who don't want lobster and hot dogs for the little kids, but for the most part, it was the same meal for everyone. But we had a lot of large groups which meant heavy trays laden with food that had to be served hot to enjoy. So someone with banquet service experience—who still wanted to do the job—was golden.

As I worked, Le Roi, our Maine Coon cat jumped into my lap and settled in like he intended to stay, purring hard. I often worked with a cat on my lap, though Le Roi was thirty pounds of muscle and fat, so he made getting anything done more challenging. Le Roi had started his life as the pet of the caretakers on Morrow Island. When they were gone, he moved into my apartment. He arrived only slightly before Chris, but he regarded Chris as an interloper, there to compete for my affection. Le Roi hid Chris's socks and his wallet. He slept crosswise on our bed, attempting to keep Chris out. Finally, when it reached the point where Chris had to check his boots in the morning before he put his feet in them, Le Roi had been exiled to Mom's. He loved her, and she him, but he still regarded me as his primary human and he visited whenever I worked in the office.

I moved Le Roi slightly and got back to work. I looked as I sorted for people who could work the clambake fire for Sonny. I wanted candidates who were out of high school at a minimum, preferably older, and physically strong. And reliable. I was looking for people who wanted full-time work because it took time to train someone and blend them into the group. I searched through the appli-cants' histories for jobs that showed evidence of these traits. With two slots empty, I wondered what the group dynamic would be when we filled the positions.

I pulled two applications out of the pile, the minimum I needed to set up the interviews for Sonny. One was a maintenance worker at Busman's Harbor High School. His hours dwindled in the summer and his schedule might well work with the clambake. Sonny might even know him. The other was a woman who worked at the local shipping store. I figured she might have the required muscle from slinging heavy boxes, and she had to be able to keep all the details straight. Neither was a slam dunk. I worried how Sonny would react to having a woman on the fire crew, but I felt encouraged.

I was nearly to the end of the applications, still search-ing, when something caught my eye. An application from Lacey Brenneman. It was written in a light-colored blue pen in a tiny, unconfident scrawl that was difficult to de-cipher. She listed her job at Great River under "previous employment" and exaggerated her time there, expanding it from two days to two months. She had even given Andie as a reference, which I thought was pretty nervy. Had she assumed I wouldn't check?

The rest of her employment history was similarly checkered, with jobs starting and ending after weeks or months, never lasting the whole season, every summer for the last three years. In addition to Andie, Lacey had offered as references a teacher at Busman's Harbor High and a woman she'd nannied for five years earlier.

There was one piece of information on the application that made my heart beat faster. I now had in my possession Lacey Brenneman's cell phone number. And a deep and burning curiosity about her relationship with Andie, and her relationship with Clark.

I called the two prospects for the clambake fire and set up their interviews with Sonny to take place in my office the next morning. They each answered their cell phones and spoke like competent adults, which was encouraging.

Then I called both Binder and Flynn and left another message on both voice mails.

Finally, I called Lacey Brenneman who also picked up right away. "Hi Lacey, I'm Julia from the Snowden Family Clambake. You dropped off an employment application at our ticket kiosk."

"Yes! Sure!" She sounded so eager I hesitated for a moment about what I planned to do. There was a zero chance I would hire her.

"Are you available for an interview?"

"Absolutely. Whenever."

"How about half an hour?" As improbable as it seemed, Lacey was, at least in my mind, a murder suspect, though it was hard to imagine her getting close enough to Andie to shove the oyster knife in her neck, much less having the strength. Nonetheless, I wanted to meet in a public place. "I see you live here in Busman's Harbor. How about Crowley's?" In the afternoon, the bar would be relatively quiet.

"Sure! I'll see you there in half an hour. How will I know you?"

"I'll wait for you at the host stand," I said.

"Perfect. See you there."

I swung by our ticket kiosk to see if more applications had been dropped off and was happy to find a dozen or so. I stashed the papers in my tote bag and went along the waterfront walkway to Crowley's.

In the late afternoon, the day had gotten colder, and a fast wind blew off the water. Lacey was already there, huddled in the open doorway, shivering into an oversized black sweater.

I greeted her and stuck out my hand. It seemed to take her a second to realize what I was doing and return the gesture. Though she said nothing, I wondered if some unconscious part of her had recognized me from the scene at the Great River Farm store.

There was no one at the host stand, so we walked in. I waved to Sam Rockmaker, who was tending his own bar. "We need a place to talk." I gestured to Lacey. "Can we sit in the back room?"

"Sure. I'll send someone along to get your order."

I led Lacey to the room she and Clark had sat in two days before. We were the only people in the huge space.

"Thank you for meeting me."

"Thank you." Lacey was wide-eyed and practically vibrating with nerves. "I really need a job."

I smiled, trying to put her at ease. "I see you have a lot of retail experience, which gives me a good sense you can deal with the public. Do you have any food service experience?"

She seemed to calm down and smiled back. "No, but I would really like to get some. I think I'd be really good at it."

The waiter showed up. Lacey and I both ordered seltzers. We were on our best behavior for the interview.

When the waiter moved off, I pressed on. "Tell me a little about yourself. Did you grow up in Busman's Harbor?" I kept my voice low. Even though the room was empty, at normal volume my voice echoed around the cavernous space.

"I graduated from Busman's Harbor High. My grandmother lived over on Union Court. I grew up at her house. My dad was a fisherman and after the fish moved on, he did, too. He left when I was a baby. I don't remember him." Lacey's face flushed red. "Is this what you want to know?" When I reassured her it was, she continued. "The reason I'm so interested in waitressing is that's what my mom does. She gets great tips."

"They don't have any open positions where your mom works?" I couldn't think of a restaurant in town that wasn't staffing up for the season.

The flush crept up her face again. "My mom and her boyfriend, they moved to Boston three years ago. The tips are great down there. My grandma died right before I graduated from high school."

I glanced at her application to remind myself of her address. I hadn't really taken it in the first time. "You live at the Ocean View Motel," I said. The Ocean View was not near the ocean and didn't have a view, a situation that had generated hundreds of angry Yelp reviews that were often quoted and joked about around town.

"I have a room there. I get up at night if someone arrives after the night clerk leaves at eleven. It doesn't happen often." Lacey hunched her shoulders and seemed to shrink into her enormous sweater. "The hours at the motel won't interfere with working at the clambake, I promise."

They wouldn't. But in addition to her jittery demeanor, Lacey's big brown eyes had deep circles under them, so dark they looked like bruises. I wondered how many times she was really up per night and if that explained her frequent absences at Great River Farm.

It was hard to connect the slight, shy, nervous mess in front of me with the girl who'd screamed so furiously at Andie. What on earth had triggered that? Lacey's was a depressingly common story. She was on her own in a small town where good-paying industries, like her father's fishing career, had gone away, and there weren't enough jobs in the off-season. She had a limited education and limited life experience, neither of which was her fault. In spite of what I knew about her, in spite of seeing her in action spitting fire at Andie Greatorex, I felt a little sorry for her.

"I noticed you didn't list Roberta Blanket as a reference." Roberta, the owner of the Ocean View Motel, was a well-known crank, who didn't believe in the internet, which was a difficult position to hold for someone in the hospitality industry in the twenty-first century.

"You can call her if you like," Lacey said. "It's just that—"

"She's difficult." I finished the sentence for her.

Lacey's shoulders relaxed. "Yes. Our arrangement works out, gives me a place to live. In the off-season it's no work at all. It's just me. I could leave town, but . . ." She stopped.

"You have a boyfriend," I supplied.

Her eyebrows flew up. The waiter returned with our

seltzers. Neither of us spoke while he set them on the table.

"I saw you in here two nights ago with a guy," I explained. "I recognized you when I arrived just now." I didn't say that I already knew who she was because of the scene at Great River. I hoped, if it dawned on her at any time that she'd seen me before, she'd assume it was because she'd seen me here, at Crowley's. But I didn't think that would happen. She'd been laser-focused on Andie at Great River and had been focused on Clark when she'd passed me the other night.

"I do have a boyfriend." She smiled at the thought.

"Tell me about him." It was a totally non-professional discussion for a job interview, but I hoped the setting, the drinks, and the confiding whisper required by the big room made it feel like we were friends having a chat.

"He's Clark. He's tall. And handsome." She giggled. "And rich."

Rich? The Clark I'd seen hanging from Pinney Kirwin's rafters hadn't looked rich. But when I thought about him, he did have the sort of casual confidence I'd associated all my life with summer kids, observations later confirmed at the fancy prep school where I'd been the weird kid who lived on an island. I wondered what Lacey, on her own at nineteen, considered "rich."

Lacey was prattling on, clearly focused on a favorite topic. "He's so nice and kind. He takes me out to dinner and he's always giving me presents."

"Do you live together at the Ocean View?"

She shook her head. "Mrs. Blanket doesn't want any one else to stay in my room. She says that's not our deal. But sometimes he does stay over." She giggled nervously.

"Where does Clark live?" Boy, was I being pushy.

But Lacey was used to being pushed around. "He lives in his family home over in Damariscotta. It's big and beautiful, right on the river."

His family home? "What's Clark's last name?"

"Kirwin. Clark Kirwin. His family is really famous for being rich."

"Clark is Pinney Kirwin's son?" I had completely misunderstood what was going on at Pinney's house.

"She's his aunt. Clark's dad is Ms. Kirwin's brother."

Chris was home when I got there. "Hey, beautiful."

Our apartment over Gus's restaurant was a studio, a huge one, but one room, nonetheless. It had a big window that overlooked the harbor, a view that would cost more than we could afford anywhere else, and alcoves for the kitchen, the closet, and the enclosed bathroom. Most of the year it was plenty big enough for both of us, since we spent so little time there, but at this particular time of the year, between seasons, I had to admit is was occasionally claustrophobic.

For years, Chris had been fixing up the cabin he'd bought from his father and it was almost done. He had vacation renters for every week of the coming summer, but after they were gone in the fall, we'd had speculative conversations about us moving there. It would be a big step, much bigger than us living together in the little studio, which still felt, after almost three years, like him staying over at my place.

We sat on our broken-down couch looking out the big window and I filled him in on my day. He listened attentively, asking the occasional question.

"What's Mack's wife like?" I asked when I'd finished.

"Ming? She's nice."

I waited. Apparently, he didn't plan to expand. "If they have two little kids already, she and Mack must have gotten together right after he and Andie broke up." I hoped to prod him to fuller disclosure. When he didn't go for it, I asked the direct question. "How did Mack and Ming meet?"

Chris furrowed his brow, clearly not appreciating the interrogation, but he answered graciously enough. "Ming worked at the restaurant. She started as a hostess, became the assistant manager, and was practically running the place while Mack was still tied up with the oyster farm."

"So Ming was there, waiting in the wings, when Mack was still with Andie."

Chris shifted and the old couch creaked in protest. "I'm not sure what you're trying to say. Ming is a nice person. You'd like her."

"I'd love to meet her."

"That would be great," he said. "If the occasion ever presents itself."

"It's presenting itself tomorrow at five-thirty," I told him. "There's a time for Andie at Mack's. I imagine Ming will be there."

CHAPTER TEN

Neither of the detectives returned my calls, but they were seated in their usual booth at Gus's the next morning and waved me over. Chris had left early for work.

"You were looking for us," Flynn said when I sat down next to Binder on the bench seat.

I filled them in with my discoveries about Clark Kirwin.

"Thanks," Binder responded. "He was on our list to interview. You've moved his priority up."

I smiled, pleased to have helped, and perhaps to have steered their focus away from Mack for a time. "Where were you guys yesterday?" I asked.

"Augusta. Autopsy." Binder swallowed a forkful of French toast. Flynn, as ever, had his little cups of soft-boiled eggs and his glass of tepid water in front of him.

"Learn anything?"

Flynn glanced at Binder, who nodded, encouraging him to fill me in.

"We learned a lot." He glanced around to make sure our neighbors were engaged in their own conversations then leaned toward me, lowering his voice. "Most important, we learned Andie Greatorex didn't die from that oyster knife shoved into her neck. She was stabbed with it post-mortem."

I was dumbfounded. "How did she die?"

"She drowned." He still hadn't opened his soft-boiled egg. "We can't be sure, but we believe her killer approached her underwater and forcibly turned off her air regulator or took off her mask."

The thought of Andie drowning in the river she loved so much was terrible. My hands went clammy, and my heart skipped a beat. "She wasn't wearing her mask when I found her. Or the hood part of the wetsuit." I pictured Andie's ponytail fanned out on top of the water. "That's one of the reasons I assumed she was attacked while she was on her dock. That and the knife," I said. "It was because she had her mask off I could tell she was dead." Andie's face with its wide-open eyes floated into my mind's eye.

"That's what we thought too, preliminarily, for the same reasons. But now we know it's not how it happened." Flynn finally tapped on the top of his egg and flipped the little shell lid off.

"If Andie died as we now think she did, it means the whole scene was staged," Binder said. "She died or became unconscious in the water, maybe wherever she was harvesting that morning. Her killer brought her to the surface, put her in a boat or some something else that floats, took her back to the dock, stabbed her in the neck with the oyster knife and made sure her body was caught on the netting so it would be discovered."

"But why?" I couldn't figure it out. "If they left her on the bottom, there would be more time to cover their tracks."

"True." Flynn drew the word out. "Unless he planned to inherit, in which case he'd want the body found quickly so he didn't have to wait for years until she was declared dead."

I couldn't make sense of it. "Maybe. But if the killer was Mack Owen, why in the world would he stick a knife with the name of his restaurant on it in her neck?"

"They were business partners and lovers," Flynn said. "Maybe he was jealous or angry. He needed to leave his mark on her in some way."

"You just one minute ago said he killed her for insurance money," I protested. "You can't have it both ways."

Binder waved his arm over the table, signaling for peace. "We have to explore every avenue." He paused. "We've searched for witnesses who saw anything on the Great River dock. Now we'll look for people who might have seen something further down the river, nearer the part of the lease where she harvested. Her boat is still missing. The Marine Patrol is searching for it. We'll talk to lobstermen, recreational boaters, the other oyster farmers, people with homes on the water. One good thing is we have a tight timeframe. Ms. Greatorex checked in with her store clerk at around nine right after he arrived. You called 911 at 10:42."

Gus returned with a mug and the coffee pot. He filled the mug for me, topped Binder's off and looked disdainfully at Flynn's tepid water. No way was he offering to get more. Binder asked for the check. Gus walked away, giving no sign whether he'd heard.

"If Andie was murdered underwater," I said. "Which one of your suspects is a skilled scuba diver?"

"An excellent question," Binder answered. "One we'll spend at least part of today trying to get an answer to."

Gus dropped the check on the table. Binder and Flynn pulled out their wallets and left cash as required. Binder picked up the bill and put it in his wallet. "I'm taking this as a receipt. May as well at least try to get reimbursed."

Gus grunted an acknowledgement, picked up the cash and walked away.

After I ordered and ate my solitary breakfast I went up to my apartment, grabbed my tote bag with the applications in it and headed to my office. As I came up the stairs, I heard Sonny's voice and one other, deep and male. I'd forgotten he was using my office for his interviews. I crept back downstairs. I hadn't been in the mood to work and it didn't take much to discourage me. I got in the Subaru and headed back to Great River Farm.

Josh was in the shop again, which surprised me. Who was going to deposit any money he collected from his sales? Who was going to sign his paycheck? Was anyone even coming to buy things? The curious could walk right down to the crime scene if they had a mind to.

I opened the door, listening to the sound of the bell over the door. Josh looked up from whatever was occupying him on the office computer. "Josh, what are you doing here?"

He rolled his shoulders. "Dunno. It doesn't seem like the farm should be left unattended. Besides, no one's turned off the WIFI and I don't have any at my place."

"Have many people been by?"

"No one. Except that Mr. Farrow. He came over to tend to the upwellers again today He showed me how to do it. He says if we don't keep the seed clean it will die. It's harder than it looks."

"That's nice of him." What was up with Ken Farrow? The seed, the oysters, the dock, the lease would all belong to Mack Owen soon enough. Maybe Farrow didn't know. I'd only heard it from Binder and Flynn, so maybe Mack's role as the heir wasn't yet general knowledge. "Did he come over on his boat or drive or what?"

"On his boat, but then he came up to the shop to get me, to teach me. He came by a lot, you know, before," Josh said.

"Ken Farrow visited often?"

"Yeah." Josh pushed his hair off his face. "He and Andie were friends. She gave him lots of advice, sold him old equipment, stuff like that. Sometimes he'd hang out here at the store even when she wasn't around."

Josh hesitated, clearly torn. Ken was acting as his surrogate boss, but something was bothering him.

"What's the matter, Josh?"

"When he came in here, he went through Andie's desk."

"He what?" It was a shocking bit of behavior even if he and Andie were friends.

"He said he was looking for bills that are due, standing orders that need to be filled, that sort of thing. But it's only been a couple of days. How could bills be that urgent? And this early in the season, it's just Andie's regular buyers and I'm sure they know . . ." His voice faltered.

"Did he take anything?" I asked.

"Not that I saw, but . . ."

"But what?"

"When he came up here, he looked through the stuff on her desk, casual-like. Then he took me down to show me how to clean the upwellers. He left me to do the last two by myself. Practice, he called it. Then he headed back to the shop. I hadn't thought to lock it when I went down to the dock. He wasn't carrying anything when he came back, but when we were done, and I returned I swear stuff was moved on Andie's desk."

"Are the desk drawers locked?"

"Yes, but the key's right here." He gestured to the bowl on the counter in front of him.

"Have the police talked to you again?"

"Not since that first day." He paled. "Should they have? Do you think there's something wrong about what Mr. Farrow is doing?"

"I don't know. Probably he's being neighborly like he said." But I sure was going to tell Binder and Flynn about this. "Did he say if orders did come in, what he was going to do about them?"

"He was going to harvest some of Andie's oysters."

"Harvest them how?"

"Diving for them, just like Andie does. Did. Why?"

It wasn't surprising Ken was a diver. He was gearing up to harvest his own oysters and he probably couldn't afford much help. But it was an interesting bit of information, nonetheless. "I'm going to leave my car here while I go next door to the Kirwins, okay?" I said.

"Course."

I opened the door, which caused the little bell to tinkle again. I was fully outside when Josh called after me. "Is Mr. Farrow going to be my boss now? Do you know?"

"If he was, how would that be?"

"He's okay, I guess. Aside from the thing with Andie's desk. That didn't feel right."

I tried to reassure him. "I'm sure things will sort themselves out. Hang in there."

He nodded. "Okay. I'm going to keep working until someone tells me to stop."

I crossed through the trees toward the Kirwin house. As I walked past Andie's cottage, I remembered how it had been rendered in the painting over Pinney's fireplace. The cottage hadn't changed a bit. It was easy to imagine Andie's farm, dock, and cottage as a part of the complex of buildings which included the sawmill and docks and structures for a robust shipbuilding operation.

I wasn't headed to the house. I'd noticed a shed near Pinney's dock. The dock itself was unremarkable, a sad remnant compared to the past. Pinney's rowboat floated there, though the oars and life jacket she had left the day before had been put away. Two kayaks and a canoe were turned upside down, their undersides bathing in the bright spring sun.

The shed on the riverbank near the dock seemed like exactly the place I would keep my scuba gear if I were Clark. I was pretty sure Pinney wouldn't be the type to allow stuff like that cluttering up the house. Assuming, of course, that Clark was a scuba diver. It didn't seem farfetched to me. Since Lacey had told me he was Pinney's brother's son, it was easy to imagine he'd been on family vacations on tropical islands with pretty reefs and ship-wrecks. It wasn't impossible.

"Julia! Miss Snowden!" I was at the shed door, ready to fling it open, my phone at the ready to photograph the evidence, when Pinney called to me. She hurried down the lawn waving her arms.

I greeted her with as brave a smile as I could muster. "Hi Pinney."

"What are you doing here?" she demanded, "Again."

"I wandered over from Great River." (True.) "I had heard the property over there used to belong to the Kir-win estate." (Also true.) "I was interested in comparing the architecture of Andie's cottage to the main house." (Sort of true. Could have been true in some alternate timeline where Andie wasn't dead, and I wasn't trespass-ing. Again.) If I wasn't completely lying, what was that tell-tale quiver in my voice?

"What were you doing by my shed?"

"I was trying to get a good vantage point to photo-graph your house. For comparison purposes." (An utter and complete lie, but I was in so deep I couldn't figure out how to escape.)

"Well." Pinney crossed her arms. As before, she was dressed in matching pastels and prints, her trademark headband on, her face made-up. "Did you get the view you hoped for?" She wasn't buying what I was selling for a minute.

"Yes. Thank you so much." I gestured with my phone. "Can I get of photo of you in front of your house?"

In her shoes I would have said no in a heartbeat, but she uncrossed her arms and gave me a tight smile. I snapped a photo. "It's true, correct? Great River, Andie's cottage and your home were all one estate."

"They were. A great estate and a thriving shipbuilding business." She was warming up a little.

"You sold part of the property to Andie and Mack."

"That wasn't my doing. I inherited the estate from my grandparents. I own it with my two brothers and three cousins. None of them have ever had the affection for the place I have. Two of the cousins have never even been here. When Great River made their offer, I objected. But the rest of the family jumped on it, and since the trust is governed by the majority, I lost out. I didn't want a fish farm next door; I can tell you that. Still don't."

"Andie told me she bought the cottage in a later transaction."

"Even more tragic, even more unwanted—by me. The rest of them couldn't wait to get their mitts on the money. Luckily, the trust retained some of the cash from that transaction for the benefit of the remaining property, though it's not nearly enough, which is why you came upon my nephew hanging from the roof the other day. We do what we can."

"Did your nephew Clark grow up spending his summers here at The Chandlery?"

"No. My brother has a big house on Cape Cod. It's only recently Clark has developed an interest in family history. He came to stay with me to soak up as much as he could. His father doesn't care. Couldn't tell him a thing. Clark's as angry we sold the property to Great River as I am."

I didn't have a response to that, and we stood in uncomfortable silence for a moment. "Thanks so much for the photo." I started to walk away, then thought better of it. "Does your nephew scuba dive, do you know?"

"Why ever would you ask me that?"

"I, um, need some dock work done and I thought since he's a handyman maybe he was looking for work." The gears in my head were turning so hard making that one up I was surprised Pinney couldn't hear them.

Pinney's smile was smug. "Clark is an avid diver as a matter of fact, but he is not currently looking for any additional assignments. I trust we won't see you on the property again."

Pinney turned and walked, stiff-backed, toward the house. Given her breeding it probably took a conscious effort to leave out the customary "Good-bye."

CHAPTER ELEVEN

It was eleven-thirty when I drove into downtown Damariscotta. I passed Mack's Shack and kept going, not turning off the main street until I got to the other side of town. I called the Damariscotta police department non-emergency line as I drove. Binder and Flynn weren't around, which didn't surprise me. The receptionist asked if I wanted to leave a message. I gave her a cheery, "No, thanks!"

I passed my uncle's house. My aunt's car wasn't in the drive. My uncle's pickup was but craning my neck I could see *My Sharona* wasn't at the dock. I turned onto the now-familiar private road that led to Midden Bay Oyster Farm and parked in front of Ken Farrow's house.

Farrow answered my knock. Behind him, Red gave me a lazy flip of his tail, not even bothering with a bark. "Ms. Snowden, what brings you here again so soon?"

"I'm still following up on Andie's robbery."

He furrowed the dark brows. "I don't understand. Following up on whose behalf? With the murder, the robbery must be the business of the police now. As it always was," he amended.

I ignored the question because I didn't have a good answer. Instead I said, "Josh at Great River tells me you were over there again today."

"What of it?"

"That was awfully neighborly of you."

"I'm a nice guy. Do you want to come in?" He asked the question as if to prove his nice guy status.

"Thanks." I breezed past him, and put a hand out for Red to sniff. "Remember me?" I patted his bumpy old head.

When we were settled in Ken's kitchen, I asked more pointedly, "Why are you helping out on Andie's farm? Shouldn't it be the heir's responsibility?"

He sat back on the hard kitchen chair. "If you're hinting around that you know who inherits, I do too. I know Mack gets Great River."

That was a surprise. "So shouldn't it be up to him to take care of the upwellers and keep the farm running? He certainly knows how. He used to co-own it."

"Mack knows I'm helping out. It's an informal arrangement. He and I have been talking about going into business together for a while. We're pals."

This was new information. "I didn't realize you were friends with Mack."

"Ayup. Mack was one of the first people I got to know when I came to town. I spent a lot of time at the restaurant, talking to him about oysters, hoping to sell some to him in the future. From there the conversations progressed into going into business together."

"What sort of business?" I asked.

"Oyster farming, of course."

"Oyster farming? Mack was already in that business. He went through a complicated business transaction, not to mention personal breakup, to get out of it."

"Turns out he misses it. He loves the restaurant, but Mack's a restless guy. He needs new worlds to conquer. He was going to invest in Midden Bay and help me expand it."

My thoughts ran in several directions. "If Mack was going to invest in your farm, does that mean he also objected to the expansion of Andie's lease?"

"'Course. He planned to speak against it at the hearing."

That wasn't a pretty picture. Mack giving public testimony against a former business partner and lover. "But the hearing is never going to happen, and now Mack owns an oyster farm." A bigger, more successful one than Ken's. "So what about your proposed partnership?"

"We haven't had a chance to talk it through. Too much has happened too quickly. But my hope is that we'll reconfigure the partnership and combine the Great River and Midden Bay holdings. I can manage the farm. Mack can't do it single-handed even with help at the restaurant. We were planning to work together anyway. That way, there's no need to pursue an expanded lease for either farm. Midden Bay gives Mack the extra area Andie wanted, and even better, there's oysters already growing. I'm not a sole proprietor anymore, but I get a smaller piece of a bigger operation. It's a win-win."

"Except for Andie."

"Except for her," he admitted. "May she rest in peace."

"Did you take anything from Andie's desk at the store?" I asked.

"What? Why would you ask me that?"

"Josh thought you had been through Andie's desk."

"He did, did he?" Farrow rubbed a hand across his chin. His white whiskers created a sandpapery sound. "No reason not to tell you. Andie had some plans to expand her dock and sorting shed to accommodate a larger farm. They were preliminary drawings. They haven't yet been filed with the planning board and the hundred other bureaucrats who get something to say when you propose building on the water. But I thought the drawings might be helpful for my conversations with Mack about combining the businesses. So I took them."

"I'm not sure you should have done that."

"Why not? The cops have already finished. There's no crime scene tape in the shop. Josh is working in there. Mack owns the plans and I'm going to be giving them to him as soon as I've finished going over them. I haven't stolen from anybody."

"Pinney Kirwin won't like the idea of a bigger operation right next door."

"No she won't. Andie would have had to fight her for both the lease expansion and the new building. Pinney should be relieved the net result is no more cages on the river. Besides," he said. "I think I can handle Pinney better than Mack or Andie could. I didn't do an underhanded deal with her relatives to buy her land out from under her."

* * *

I chewed over what Ken had told me as I drove to my aunt and uncle's house. Andie's murder had Ken Farrow sitting pretty much in clover. He was partners with Mack, or at least he hoped to be, in a larger, more sustainable, profitable operation. He didn't have to fight Andie's lease expansion or try to get a bigger lease of his own. He didn't have to raise a lot of oysters from scratch and wait three years for the payoff.

On the other hand, what Ken had told me made Mack look pretty terrible, too. If Mack wanted to get back in the oyster farming business, Andie's murder had handed that to him on a platter. Inheriting Great River was a windfall for Mack in more ways than one.

My Sharona wasn't at the dock, but I was hopeful. Lobstermen start their days before dawn. My uncle was frequently home by early in the afternoon.

I walked around to the back of the house and climbed the stairs to the deck. It was a little chilly for sitting out, so I went to my car and grabbed my emergency Snowden Family Clambake sweatshirt from the back. Then I settled into the old glider swing on the deck to wait.

My uncle showed up at around two o'clock, as he had the last time I'd been there. He saw me as he carefully docked *My Sharona* and gave a little wave. He unplugged the depth finder, GPS, and radio from the console and headed for the shed. I walked down the lawn to meet him.

"Hey, Julia. You're getting to be like the proverbial bad penny." He put the equipment on the ground, fished a key ring from the pocket of his lobsterman's coveralls and put it in the padlock.

"I was in town again." Not much of an explanation, but he didn't push for a better one.

He swung the old wooden door open and bent to pick up the depth finder. Then he stopped, his big torso still perpendicular to the ground, his head aimed straight into the shed. "What the—" He stood with the fluid movement of a much younger man and slammed the shed door closed.

"What?" I moved toward him. "What is it?"

"Don't look in there!" He pushed his full weight against the door.

My heart banged. There had already been one murder in town. What had he seen that was causing him to freak out? "Uncle Bob, move!"

He stepped back, shaking his head. I opened the door.

Inside the shed was a wetsuit, large enough to cover my uncle's ample body, a mask, and a tank. I was so transfixed by them; I almost didn't see the thing that had caused my uncle to panic. But there they were, front and center—two empty plastic pails, one inside the other. Visible on the bottom one were the stenciled words GREAT RIVER.

I shut the shed and led Uncle Bob toward the house. I called Flynn as we walked. For once, he picked up.

"Julia."

"Sergeant. I'm at my uncle's house. You need to come over here. We've found Andie Greatorex's missing oyster seed pails."

"Where?"

"In his shed."

Flynn hesitated. "We're tied up. Wait a sec." He could send a local cop or a state trooper to pick the pails up and question my uncle. But they were connected to an active murder investigation. "One of us will be over. It may take a while."

"We'll wait."

"I never did anything to Andie." Uncle Bob sat heavily in his chair at the kitchen table, his routine of showering and changing before he came upstairs completely forgotten.

"Of course you didn't. But how do you think those pails got in your shed?"

"I wish I had a clue. I have never seen them before this very moment."

His reaction had seemed genuine. He'd been shocked, no question. "They weren't there this morning, I swear. I got my gear and went to my boat, just like every other morning.

"Is the shed always locked?"

"Yes, always." Then he hesitated. "But there's a spare key in case I don't have my set with me."

Geez. Most people in our area didn't lock the doors to their homes, much less their outbuildings. Mom's unlocked house doors had been a bone of contention between the two of us for years. "Where do you keep this extra key?"

"On the ledge over the shed door."

Where anyone could get it. But maybe that was better. Better anyone than no one except my uncle. Sometime today, someone had come and put those incriminating pails in my uncle's shed. Why? Two things were clear. Whoever did it wasn't just getting rid of evidence; they were planting it. To make Uncle Bob look bad. "Who out there would be interested in making you a suspect?"

"What?" He seemed genuinely astonished by the question.

"Someone did this in an attempt to frame you for Andie's murder. Or at the very minimum to cause you trouble with the police. Who would that have been and why?"

"I don't have an enemy on this earth. I swear it."

I didn't believe him for a second. "Uncle Bob, there's not a lobsterman alive who can genuinely say that." It was a territorial business of sharp elbows and big egos. It attracted people who wanted to be the captains of their own ships, the masters of their fate. It was not for the faint of heart.

"Hello!" The front door opened, and my aunt trudged into the hall, laden with canvas tote bags of papers to mark and lessons to prepare. "Why are you sitting—" She caught sight of my uncle. He'd removed his jacket and boots while we'd talked, he was still in his bright orange oilskin overalls. "Bob."

"Come in. Sit down." He explained to her what had happened. When he said, "A state police detective is on the way," my aunt's jaw, already open, dropped further.

"Did you see anyone hanging around this morning before you left for school?" I asked her. "In the yard or on the street?"

"No one. But I think I know who did it. It was that Ken Farrow."

"Why do you say that?" Uncle Bob was abrupt, almost angry. Like Andie, he hadn't been able to think of his life in terms of having enemies.

"Because he walks that dog along the river and cuts through our yard. I see them out there all the time."

"But not this morning," I said.

"No," she admitted. "But regularly enough he'd know about the shed, know where the key was."

The key wasn't exactly in a genius hiding place. Anyone could have found it. I kept that thought to myself.

"But why?" Bob demanded. "Why put those pails my shed?"

"That I don't know," my aunt conceded.

"Have you done anything to antagonize him? Did you vandalize his cages? Mess with his gear?" I asked.

"I told you we never did nothing like that."

My aunt put a steadying hand on his arm. "Bob." Her voice held a warning.

"Okay. Okay. We didn't want those oyster farms expanding. New ones like Farrow's are as bad as bigger ones like Andie's. We may have done a few things. Over the years."

"Did you target Midden Bay or Great River specifically?" I asked. Next to me, my aunt drew in a noisy breath and held it.

"Never." My uncle put a hand up, oath-taking style.

"Did you or any of the others escalate the activity against Great River recently, maybe to register your objection to her lease application?"

"No!" The word exploded out of my uncle's mouth.

"Why us?" my aunt asked. "Why would Ken leave the pails in our shed?"

"To get suspicion off him." My uncle's face was the color of a boiled lobster. "He had to get rid of the pails and why not use them to make someone else look guilty? He probably knew the police had talked to me already."

"Or, it could be as simple as he knew where the key to your shed was," I said. "It could have been all about opportunity."

When Flynn showed up, we walked him through what had happened. He wasn't a jerk about it, didn't treat my uncle like a suspect, which I appreciated. He listened when my aunt, in answer to a direct question, told him that she'd often seen Ken Farrow in the yard. Flynn's face betrayed nothing. We walked out to the shed where he put on gloves and picked up the pails. He gave the scuba gear a long look, but said nothing about it.

"You'll both need to come to the station to give formal statements," he said to my aunt and uncle. "Now, if possible."

Aunt Sharon and Uncle Bob agreed, still looking shell-shocked.

"I'll walk with you." I followed Flynn back to his un-marked car. "I happen to have talked to Ken Farrow this afternoon," I told him.

"Have you now," he responded.

I filled him in on my conversation while he put the pails in a big, clear plastic bag and placed them in his trunk.

Flynn closed the trunk with a thunk. "So Farrow ends up at the end of this with a partnership in a bigger, ongoing enterprise and Owen gets back in the oyster farming business," he said when I was done. He went around to the driver's side, got in, started the car, and rolled down the window.

"Don't you dare say win-win," I said.

"Julia, a woman is *dead*. How could I ever call that a win?"

By that time my aunt and uncle had come out to the driveway. Uncle Bob had changed out of oilskins into a worn pair of jeans. They climbed into my aunt's car. She was on the driver's side, which showed how shaken my uncle was. He was normally the family driver. I went over to say good bye. "By the way," I said to my uncle. "When did you start diving?"

"Diving?" He looked puzzled.

"The scuba gear in the shed," I reminded him.

"Oh, that. I got my certification ages ago. It comes in handy for untangling lines under the boat. I wear the wetsuit sometimes when I'm working in the water. But I haven't dived in ages. Why?"

"Just curious," I lied and headed toward my car.

I barely made it back to Busman's Harbor in time to meet Chris and get changed before we returned to Damariscotta and Andie's "time."

CHAPTER TWELVE

We drove to Damariscotta in Chris's truck. On the ride over, I told him about the discovery of Andie's pails in my uncle's shed and my conversation with Ken Farrow.

He grunted, not saying anything. I was sure he was happy for any trail that led away from Mack, but his mind was on Andie. The tightness of his jaw convinced me he wasn't looking forward to the memorial. We lapsed into silence for the rest of the ride.

The parking lot at Mack's Shack was packed even though it was only a few minutes past five-thirty. In Maine, being on time meant you were late. When we finally found a spot on the street, Chris came around to the passenger side of the pickup to help me down from the high seat and gave me a hug as I slid into his arms.

"Ready for this?" His voice was low and thick with emotion.

"As I'll ever be."

I grabbed his hand and gave it a squeeze.

Inside, Mack's was crowded and noisy. People talked loudly and greeted one another with handshakes and hugs. Andie's friends and neighbors had gathered to trade stories and find strength and solace in each other's company.

"Hello!" Mack clasped Chris's outstretched hand and pulled him in for a hug. Chris surprised me standing chest to chest with Mack for a long moment. "I am so sorry," he said to Mack.

"I know." Mack's voice was ragged. But then he rallied and gave me a hug as well. "It's a cash bar. Sorry, I couldn't swing anything else, even for Andie. But there's plenty of food. Help yourselves." Mack waved his arm in an expansive fashion, taking in the whole of the restaurant. "My wife is around here somewhere. The poker friends are here, too."

I spotted my aunt and uncle at a large table in the center of the room surrounded by local lobstering friends. Uncle Bob smiled and waved us over. For the most part, he didn't seem any the worse for wear for his ordeal of the afternoon. He turned in his seat as Chris and I approached. Aunt Sharon stared at Chris. I was used it. His looks had that kind of effect on people, especially women-people.

"Ladies and gents." Uncle Bob raised his voice to be heard over the conversations taking place around the table. "My niece Julia Snowden. Julia, are you going to introduce us to your friend?"

I blushed slightly. "Everyone, this is Chris Durand.

Chris, this is my Aunt Sharon, my dad's sister, and her husband Bob. And their friends."

Chris reached his hand out. Uncle Bob took it, even though he remained seated. "Pull up a chair, pull up a chair," Bob said.

Chris found two empty chairs at a nearby table and brought them over. When I was seated, he said, "I'm going to the bar. White wine?"

"Please."

"Anybody need anything?" he asked the table at large.

"All set," people chorused back. From the number of beer bottles collecting on the table, along with piles of empty oyster shells, it appeared they were.

"We were talking about Andie," my uncle said.

"Cunning girl," a skinny man said. In most English-speaking places, cunning meant smart or sneaky. In Maine it meant cute or adorable. It was an expression applied more to children and puppies than grown women. I couldn't imagine anyone saying it about Andie when she was alive. But death often knocks off the edges.

"Lovely," the skinny man's wife said. She wore a sweatshirt that said, "World's Best Bass Fisher." In Maine, you might dress for a funeral, but you don't dress up for a "time."

"She knew the water, that Andie," another man said. "Made a real go of that farm."

Everyone nodded in agreement. I focused on keeping my thoughts from showing on my face. Only a few hours before, my uncle had confessed that these people were responsible for vandalizing the oyster farmers' gear. But as they went around the table, reminiscing, I came to believe they respected Andie and felt the loss. Andie had said they never did anything that cost her money, though her crop was vulnerable to being stolen or destroyed. These were good people, worried about their way of life, who were simply letting the farmers, and world, know "We're still here."

"It started with the robbery," the skinny man said. His voice was too deep for his size. It sounded like the low thrum of a cement mixer. "Did the cops ever figure out what happened with that?"

My uncle reddened but didn't say a word. My aunt stared at her beer glass. They hadn't told their friends about finding Andie's pails in their shed. Normally an adventure like that would be shared eagerly. Perhaps someday it would be. Once Andie's killer was caught.

My aunt rose and left the table. I worried she was uncomfortable with the conversation. Then, out of the corner of my eye, I saw she had waylaid Chris as he made his way back to the table with a beer bottle in one hand and my wine in the other.

One lobsterman put up both hands, palms forward. "It wasn't any of us."

"Darn right," another man at the table said. "'Course it wasn't. None of us would have robbed Andie, much less hurt her."

"What would any of us have done with a couple of buckets of oyster seed?" a third man said. "Put it in the home aquarium?"

That brought some laughter and a general lessening of tension around the table. The skinny man took a swig of beer and several others followed suit.

My aunt and Chris still stood fifteen feet away. The room was full of people and buzzy conversation. I couldn't hear was being said, but it was clear she was interrogating him. He needed to be rescued.

"Excuse me," I said to Uncle Bob and the table at large. "I'm going to grab my wine. So nice to meet everyone."

There was a general mumble of "Nice to meet yous" as I pushed back my chair and hurried toward Chris.

When I'd worked my way through the crowd to his side, he smiled at me benevolently. He knew what I was up to. "Your aunt was telling me some stories about you as a child." He had to shout so I could hear him.

Great. "I'm sure none of them are true," I shouted back.

"Remember that time, Julia, when you ate so much *Good & Plenty* you threw up in the movie theater?" My aunt wrinkled her nose mischievously.

I did remember. "Look, food! See you later Aunt Sharon." I grabbed Chris's hand and pulled him to the buffet table.

"Is that why you never eat licorice?" he asked. "Because when I offered you those black jellybeans we bought to put in Page's Easter basket that time—"

"Yeah, yeah, yeah. Changing the subject. Look at this spread." I gestured at the buffet. "You hungry?"

He was. On the table were martini glasses filled with pink mashed potatoes, garnished with a green olive stuffed with pimento. I reached for one. "Yum. Lobster mashed." I offered Chris a taste from my fork which he accepted gratefully.

"Mack has trained every chef who's ever worked here." Chris had picked up a small, square plate. The food on it was beautifully composed, chunks of pink tuna garnished with avocado, cucumber, sesame seeds, chopped jalapeño pepper, and cilantro. "Fantastic." He held the plate out to me.

"Is the tuna raw?"

"Cooked," he answered. "You have to get over this new thing you have about raw seafood."

"I ate the oysters, didn't I?" I took my fork and dug in. The flavors that exploded in my mouth were amazing. Warm, spicy, and cool. Sweet and vinegary. Crunchy and pleasantly chewy. A great mouthfeel, foodies would say.

The rest of the buffet was laden with gorgeous hors d'oeuvres: Baked oysters, puff pastries, shrimp cocktail, miniature cups of chowder, and of course, nearby on the oyster bar, hundreds of raw oysters, open and inviting.

"Quite a spread," I said.

"Mack wouldn't do anything less for Andie," Chris said. "That's why the idea that he might have killed her for money or for Great River is ridiculous."

I scanned the room looking for people I knew. Josh from the Great River store was sitting at a table with a group of young people I thought might be current and former co-workers. Ken Farrow approached and shook Josh's hand, nodding as Josh introduced him and sat down with the others. He was ingratiating himself with the help no doubt, the folks he hoped would soon work for him.

Across the room I spotted Pinney Kirwin sitting at a table with Lacey Brenneman. I'd expected Pinney, if she were even there, to be sitting at a table with other summer people. It wasn't strange to break bread, or in this case to sip wine, with your nephew's girlfriend, but Lacey, the girl who made ends meet by managing a motel in exchange for a room, didn't seem like Pinney's cup of tea. And where was Clark? If they were together, I'd have expected it to be the three of them, not two. I considered going over to say hello to Pinney and Lacey, but I didn't want them comparing notes about their conversations with me.

I realized Chris was no longer beside me. Craning my neck, I searched the room. He was in the opposite corner, his back to me, talking to Sam Rockmaker, Mack, and a group of people, I guessed they were the poker players and their significant others. I moved closer, hoping he'd turn around and invite me over. I had just decided to crash the little group when a woman materialized next to me.

"You must be Julia. I'm Ming, Mack's wife."

She'd come up on me so suddenly I was startled. "Yes, of course." I spotted two little girls playing nearby. They were adorable, maybe three and two, dressed in identical smocked dresses with sailboats embroidered on them.

I would have said Ming was as different from Andie as two women could be. Andie was tall and broad-shouldered, physically dominating. I couldn't imagine her in a dress. Ming was petite, a miniature bundle of energy, dressed in a flowing handkerchief dress with an asymmetrical hem. Yet both women emanated a sense of confidence, of being in command. Maybe Mack Owen did have a type.

"I'm so pleased to meet you," I said. "I love your restaurant. It's a perfect place, casual, yet elevated. Relaxed and impressive at the same time. You must be very proud."

Ming smiled, gazing at the crowded tables and the people standing in groups, her children playing peek-a-boo around the guests' legs. "Thank you. We are proud. It means a lot to me that you say that. Your family has run a successful business on the midcoast forever. I haven't been to the clambake for years, but I remember a trip there when I first moved to town nine years ago. It was a wonderful afternoon, like you say, relaxed and casual yet still very special. A feast for the eyes, ears, nose, and taste buds."

"Thank you. I wasn't living in Maine back then. My parents were running the clambake, before my dad died," I said.

"I know. You were in New York City, working in venture capital."

I didn't wonder how she knew that. Chris must have told Mack who told her. But why had he told his friends so much about me, and never mentioned a word about them to me?

"Have you been in our restaurant before?" Ming asked.

"Twice, but both times were in the last few days, once before Andie died, and once after."

"Mack told me Chris asked you to help Andie figure out who robbed her. Chris must have been really worried about Andie. Turns out he was right."

"Yes." Apparently, I was the subject of more than occasional discussion, though I noticed Mack apparently hadn't told her he asked for my help. We edged our way over toward the oyster bar. Two employees behind it were shucking as fast as they could, and the oysters were disappearing just as fast. There was a Great River sign, though it marked only an empty bed of ice. I thought it was a touching tribute to Andie and I told Ming so.

"What?" At first, she didn't seem to understand what I'd said. Then she followed my gaze to the Great River sign. "That wasn't empty," she said. "Ken harvested a bunch of Great Rivers today. Everyone agreed it was a fitting tribute. We must have run out."

We were silent for a moment as we watched the crowd. I was shocked to see Clark Kirwin, wearing a busboy's jacket in Mack Shack's trademark blue, clearing the table where my aunt and uncle and their friends sat. He wore rubber gloves and placed the plates and beer glasses in a bin.

"Clark Kirwin works here?" I didn't hide my surprise.

"He turned up earlier in the spring. Thank goodness for him. He's good at almost everything that needs to be done in the restaurant. Mack has really come to rely on him. Don't be surprised if you come back this summer and Clark is hosting or waiting or even in the kitchen cooking."

"I thought he worked for his aunt fixing up the place."

Ming looked pointedly at Pinney's table. Clark had moved over there and was chatting with his aunt and girlfriend while he cleared their dishes. "I'm sure Pinney is getting every spare minute out of Clark that she can. But she's not going to pay him, is she?"

We were quiet again. There was so much I wanted to ask her about Mack and Andie, and about Chris. I couldn't figure out how.

It was Ming who broke the silence. "I want you to know," she said, "the fact that we've never met is not for lack of trying. We've invited Chris to bring you along numerous times when the gang was doing stuff, especially to couples' night at poker."

Couples' night? Heat surged into my cheeks and I must have glowed bright red from the neck up. But I was too embarrassed to ask about the details of couples' night. Too embarrassed and too angry.

Ming was still talking. "I don't want you to think we're rude. Or snobs. Or we think we own Chris. He's always been reluctant . . ." She caught the look on my face and let the rest of the sentence drift.

I didn't know what to say. What could I have said, even if I'd been capable of speech? I finally managed a, "Thank you for telling me," in a shaky voice that was two octaves too high and fled to the ladies' room.

I stayed in the stall too long, taking deep breaths to get my heart rate down. What the heck was going on? In Busman's Harbor, I couldn't have been more visible as Chris's girlfriend. We ran a restaurant together for Pete's sake. But forty minutes away, in Damariscotta, I was some kind of secret lover, meant to be kept in the closet, never displayed. Why?

Eventually I calmed down. I knew I had to come out of the bathroom sometime. Maybe Chris would even start looking for me at some point. I left the ladies' room and edged into the crowd.

As I entered the room from one side, Lieutenant Binder and Sergeant Flynn came through the door into the restaurant. I was so happy to see them I almost cried.

I made my way across the crowded floor toward the state police detectives. I wanted to tell them Clark Kirwin was connected not only to Andie's angry ex-employee Lacey Brenneman, to Pinney Kirwin, his aunt, but also to Mack Owen, his employer. Mack had asked for my help, but I'd warned him I wouldn't hide anything from the police. Besides, they would know soon enough when Clark returned to the dining room with his busboy's bin.

I finally made to their side of the room. "Lieutenant—"

"Friends." Mack Owen stood in the center of the floor with a handheld microphone. "Thank you all for being here tonight."

"Thank you for the spread!" a man shouted. There was a round of applause.

"We're all here because we loved Andie. Our community is so much less without her. I thought we could say a few words. I'll start and then pass the mic."

Mack stood up straighter and began. "As many of you know, I met Andie in college. I knew she was special instantly. She had an energy, a drive, an ambition that was infectious. She knew what she wanted and what she wanted was oysters. Before I knew what had happened to me, that's what I wanted, too. We founded Great River together, an enduring contribution that makes our beloved river, our town, and the world a better place. It's an accomplishment I will always be proud of." He held out his arm and Ming went to his side. The two little girls followed and wrapped themselves around their parents' legs.

My eyes welled up at the sight of them. I'd run such a range of emotions since I'd arrived at Mack's, embarrassed by my aunt, furious at Chris for keeping his friends out of our life together, my mind working away on the puzzle of Andie's death, and sadness for missing out on knowing Andie, who had been special indeed.

"And that's why," Mack said, "I'm announcing today, Ming and I will be keeping Great River and farming it as a family. Andie left it to me, to us. It was her greatest achievement and most prized possession. We will honor her by keeping the farm running." He leaned down and picked up the smaller of the girls. She clung to his side, a little intimidated by the crowd, a serious expression on her face. "I hope one day I can pass the farm on to my children."

The speech was followed by serious applause. I tugged on Flynn's sleeve to indicate I needed to talk, but he shook his head. The mic had been passed, and he and Binder stood in polite silence.

My uncle stood and spoke with warmth and respect about Andie and her love for the river. Josh spoke movingly about how much he had learned from her and how great she had been as a boss. I thought it took a lot of courage for him to stand in front of the crowd, as young and reserved as he was, and his bravery brought another tear to my eye. Sam Rockmaker spoke for the poker players. He got the crowd laughing with stories of Andie's outrageous bidding. Other people I didn't know spoke too, former employees, chefs who were devoted customers, fellow oyster farmers. Through it all, Binder and Flynn stood still and looked respectfully on.

When the speeches finished, Ming took the microphone and thanked everyone. She urged us all to stay on. The crowd surged toward the bar. I looked around for Chris and couldn't find him. I didn't see Mack or Ken, either. Clark Kirwin had taken off his busboy's jacket and was seated at the table with his girlfriend and his aunt.

"I need to talk to you," I told Binder and Flynn. "About the case. It's important. Clark Kirwin," I nodded in Kirwin's direction. "He is at the center of this, I'm convinced. He's connected to—"

Someone bumped against my back. "Not here," Flynn hissed.

The room was full. "We can talk in Mack's office. It's at the back." I led them down the narrow passageway. The office door was ajar, and a sliver of light from inside fell across the dark wood of the hallway floor.

"This is an outrage!"

I turned to Binder and Flynn and mouthed, "Ken Farrow." Binder gave me a quick nod. He'd recognized Farrow's voice.

The oyster farmer was shouting. "We had a deal. I was going to go after an expanded lease, and you were going to fund me. It was all agreed. All I had to do was make sure Andie didn't get approved."

Mack's voice was shaky. "I don't think that's what we said, exactly, Ken. We said, casually, that if Andie didn't get the lease expansion, there might be an opportunity for someone else. And I may have said I regretted getting out of farming and was looking for another opportunity."

"*May* have said!" Farrow as livid. "It was *arranged*."

"Ken." Mack's tone was intended to placate, but also held a warning. "Whatever we may have," he hesitated, "speculated about, surely you can see it doesn't make sense for me now. I own a farm. A really good one. I don't need to invest in another."

There was silence for a moment. "Then hire me to run it," Farrow said. "You've got the restaurant. Ming's home with the girls. Cut me in. Combine Great River and Midden Bay. Let me manage the whole shebang."

"Ming's going to come back and run the restaurant." Mack's voice was calm. "It's been decided. I'll run the farm. We don't need you or Midden Bay, Ken. It doesn't make sense."

"You owe me." There was a threat in Farrow's voice.

"Why do I owe you?" Mack was curious, unconcerned. But when Farrow didn't answer the tone shifted. "*Ken, what did you do?*"

I felt movement behind me. Binder touched my shoulder and whispered in my ear. "You need to get out of here, Julia."

When I opened my mouth to protest, Flynn turned me around and gave me a gentle shove down the passageway.

I never did get to tell them about Clark Kirwin.

CHAPTER THIRTEEN

The cab of Chris's truck was silent on the way home. Chris was relaxed, hands loose on the wheel as he drove down Route 1. It wasn't the fastest way back to Busman's Harbor, but locals avoided the more direct route along the River Road at night due to the deer. My mother had hit one years earlier, and I'll never forget the look on my dad's face when he escorted her into the house after he picked her up. She was white and later sore from where the seatbelt had stopped her body's forward motion. He was undone, shaking, unable to speak. Later he told us when he'd seen the dead buck on the hood of her car, its antlers inches from the windshield, he'd had a glimpse of what life would be like without her. At the time, I couldn't imagine either one of them without the other, but now my mother had gone on for seven years alone. After a long and rocky period, she was back, participating in her life.

In the darkness on the empty road, my mind lurched from topic to topic. Clark, connected to Lacey, Pinney, and Mack. Ken Farrow, harvesting oysters from the Great River beds in scuba gear. And later, implying to Mack Owen that they'd had some sort of a deal. It didn't sound good for Ken, and it didn't sound good for Mack, who had admitted he wanted to get back into the oyster farming business. Now he was.

I tried and failed to untie the knots. I tried to have it all add up to clearing Mack, but I couldn't get there.

Pinging onward, my mind reviewed my conversation with Ming Owen. "We've invited Chris to bring you along numerous times when the gang was doing stuff, especially to couples' night at poker," she'd said.

I broke the silence. "Why didn't you ever invite me to couples' night at poker?"

Chris took a moment to answer. "I guess I didn't think you'd enjoy it."

"Whatever gave you that idea?" I was geared up for an argument.

"Well," he drew the word out in a way that only angered me more, "I've never seen you play cards."

"I play cards," I said. "You never asked me." This was only a slight exaggeration. I have played cards. If you counted cutthroat games of War with my sister Livvie during rainy afternoons on Morrow Island when we were kids. "Are you embarrassed by me? Why didn't you want me to meet your friends?"

"Julia." His hands tightened on the steering wheel and he tapped the brake though there wasn't a car in sight, perhaps, subconsciously, trying to put a brake on the conversation. "I have never been embarrassed by you. Ever. I think you know that."

I did, at some deeper level, but the part of me that was the middle school outcast while he was a handsome high school senior had taken hold. "Why all the secrets then? First, you don't tell me about your family. Then you don't introduce me to your friends." My voice grew thick. I had tears in my eyes. "I don't understand."

Chris took the turn onto the two-lane highway that led down the peninsula to Busman's Harbor. "I'm sorry," he said. "I've explained about my family. I can't apologize about it again. Either you accept it, or you don't. I don't know why I haven't invited you to do things with my friends. We live together. We work together the entire off-season. Maybe I wanted to preserve some part of my old life that was just mine."

By then I really was crying. "I've let you into my whole life," I said. "You've become a part of my family. You've spent every holiday with us since we've been together. Page and Jack think you're their uncle." I took a deep breath to stop the tears. It didn't work.

Chris didn't speak again until we were halfway down the peninsula. "You've shared your Maine life with me," he said, his voice low. "But I don't know anything about your life before that. I've never met any of your friends from school or New York."

"That's hardly the same. Your poker friends *are* your Maine friends." I had started off hurt and embarrassed that Ming knew so much about me and I knew nothing about her. Other conversations came back to me. Andie saying, "So glad to *finally* meet you." Mack saying, "Chris's Julia. At last."

I was furious. "I've had it, Chris. I've had it with the

lying, the hiding. I'm done with the secrets, the compart-
ments where you keep the stuff you don't want me to see.
I want to have a life together. Or a life apart. You decide.
Let me in or leave me out. Completely."

He pulled the truck into the parking lot behind Gus's
and stopped. "Julia, I'm doing my best."

"Not good enough." I pushed the door open and lowered my feet to the ground. *What now?*

"I'll sleep on the *Dark Lady* tonight," Chris said from
deep inside the cab. The sailboat had been his summer
home before he'd moved in with me.

"You do that." I slammed the truck door.

He waited until I'd fumbled with the lock and got the
door open. Once I was safely inside, he drove away.

CHAPTER FOURTEEN

The next morning I was in my office when Sonny arrived. Chris hadn't come home, or called or texted. It wasn't the first bump in our relationship, but it was our first big fight, and the first time we'd stayed apart by choice instead of circumstance. I was meant to be working, but I kept turning it over in my head. I was angry, I was embarrassed, but most of all I was scared. What did this mean for the life I'd created in Busman's Harbor? Chris had been a part of it from the beginning. He'd been part of the reason I'd stayed in town after the first crazy summer spent rescuing my family's clambake business. A big part of the reason, I had to admit.

Sonny knocked on the doorframe to my office. His big knuckles sounded like five jackhammers working simultaneously. "What's up?" He stared across the room. "You look terrible."

"I didn't sleep. How did your interviews go yesterday?"

"I got one live one, Walter, who works at the high school. He has two other offers for the summer, but he wants to work outside, and he wants to work with a crew. I think he's leaning toward us."

"Offer him another dollar an hour if it will seal the deal. What about the woman?" I had wondered how Sonny would react to a female member of his crew.

"No-showed." He put both palms out in a gesture that might have meant, "Whaddya going to do?" or "Figures."

"Great." So that was that. I pulled a pile of paper from the tote bag, forgotten since the day before yesterday. "I picked up some more applications. Do you want to go through them?"

He rolled his broad shoulders. "Nah. You do it. That way you can look to fill the other positions as well. I'm going out with Dad to set traps."

Sonny's dad was a lobsterman. Hip and shoulder problems now required that one of his sons go out with him on every trip. This time of year they'd be putting out more traps, anticipating the summer, when demand increased and when the lobsters shed, creating the more sought-after soft shells. When the lobsters would shed was anyone's guess. It depended on the water temperature and other factors known only to the lobsters. It might be June or August, but Sonny's dad would want to have traps in all his traditional spots well before then so no one else could claim them.

Sonny left and I pulled the pile of applications in front of me. There were only a dozen or so. I started from the top. The first three had other seasonal jobs and were hoping for some hours to fill in around them. I couldn't see how any of their schedules could work. One said specifically she wanted to work in the gift shop, which was my mother's job.

I stared at the forms, willing myself not to feel discouraged. My head pounded. I'd gulped down some dry cereal while standing up, leaning against the sink in my tiny kitchen. I hadn't felt like facing the crowd at Gus's alone. In my head I heard Gus asking, "Where's your other half?" A question I profoundly didn't wish to answer.

Binder and Flynn wouldn't have been at Gus's in any case. They would have got an early start this morning interviewing—or maybe more accurately interrogating—Mack Owen and Ken Farrow. I never got to see this part of their work, but it was easy to picture the two detectives—Binder, the good guy, the smiling, reasonable bureaucrat who simply wanted to listen to your answers, no matter how specious, get the paperwork done, and get home to his family. Flynn, radiating menace like a viper ready to strike, would be the bad guy, the one who didn't believe a word you said, and who pushed you harder and farther than you ever intended to go.

My mom had a fancy coffee machine and I figured that was what I needed. I went down the back stairs to the kitchen, ground the beans, fetched the water, got the whole thing going, and settled down to wait. The smell was heaven. I loved the smell of coffee more than I loved the taste, though the tiny hammers in my temples reminded me I needed to drink the stuff to cure what ailed me. I brought my phone with me, in case Chris called, but I willed myself not to pick it up unless it rang.

"That smells lovely." My mother entered the kitchen. She was dressed for work in a periwinkle blue dress and scruffy green cardigan she'd remove when she got to the store. She had a few more weeks at Linens and Pantries before she took leave for the summer to work full-time at the Snowden Family Clambake gift shop.

The coffee machine shuddered to a stop. Mom glanced at me where I sat at the battered old table and then took two coffee cups out of the cupboard and poured for both of us. "You don't look so great," she said.

I'd already decided not to tell my family anything about what was going on with Chris. The fight might be a blip. He might arrive at my door the next day, the next hour, the next minute, begging to be forgiven and promising we'd have an open and honest relationship from that moment forward. If that happened, I didn't want my family referring to "that time Chris hurt Julia," for months or years afterward. If that was even what they would do. At times I suspected the whole gang of them preferred his company to mine.

So, wisely, I said nothing. Nonetheless, my mother clearly sensed something was wrong. She put milk in the cups and brought me my coffee. She sat across from me though she was clearly on her way out.

I guzzled the coffee, missing the flavor entirely, hoping the caffeine would do its work. "Busy time of year. Hiring. You know."

She did know. She'd run the business with my father for twenty-five years. And she wasn't buying what I was selling for a minute. "Didn't Chris know that oyster farmer who was murdered?" she asked.

"Yes, he did. I met her a few times too." I felt terrible using Andie's death as an excuse for my apparent sadness.

"I'm sorry," Mom said. "Tell Chris I send my condolences to him, too." She drained her cup and stood to go. "When's the last time you went out to Morrow Island?"

"Everything's ready to open," I answered, a little too snippily. "Sonny, Chris and I worked out there all of April." We'd cleaned up after the winter storms, put the picnic tables out on the lawn, and scrubbed down the little kitchen where Livvie and her small crew put out the chowder that started the clambake meal and the blueberry grunt swimming in vanilla ice cream that ended it.

"That's not what I meant." Mom's tone didn't contain a hint of rebuke, and believe me, I was looking for it. "I meant, it's a beautiful day and you look like you could stand to get your head clear."

The whole "you look terrible," thing was wearing thin. I'd glanced in the mirror that morning while I brushed my hair, like I always did. I hadn't noticed that I looked like a monster or anything.

"Go out to the island," my mother urged. "Check on Windsholme. Sit in the sun."

My mother, the New Yorker who had become the quintessential New Englander, never told either me or Livvie to take time off. Her prescription for anything that ailed you was work. "Put your shoulder to the wheel. Get something accomplished. You'll feel better," she always said. I must have looked dire.

I decided to take her up on it.

My phone buzzed, gyrating on the tabletop. My heart skipped a beat.

"I'll leave you to it," Mom said and exited through the back door.

*   *   *

I didn't recognize the phone number. "Hello?" I hoped the disappointment didn't come through in my voice.

"Ms. Snowden. It's Marty Flanaghan."

I searched my memory. Despite the name, the speaker was clearly a woman. "How can I help you, Ms. Flanaghan?"

"I hoped we could reschedule my interview."

The penny dropped. "You were supposed to meet with my brother-in-law, Sonny Ramsey, yesterday."

"I was."

I waited for the excuse. I'm a big believer in second chances, but if Marty Flanagan wanted one, she was going to have to tell me why she no-showed.

"Did you fill the position?" Marty's voice was tentative, feeling me out.

"We're still looking."

"I thought you might have filled it when no one answered the door."

"I'm sorry, did you say, no one answered the door?" Light began to dawn.

"I rang the doorbell and then I knocked and knocked. I stood on the porch, and then I sat in one of your chairs for half an hour. I thought maybe Mr. Ramsey was running late."

"I am so sorry. I'm not sure what happened." I had a very good idea about what must have happened. "I'll speak to Sonny and we'll set another time."

"Thank you so much." The woman sounded so sincere. "I didn't want to miss my chance. I've heard so many great things about working at the Snowden Family Clambake."

I promised to call her back and we hung up. "Sonny!" My shout echoed through the empty house. There was no point in calling while he was out on his dad's boat. Even if he answered, which was unlikely, it was no way to have the conversation.

I ran upstairs and swept the applications off the desk into my tote bag. I thought I might sit out on one of our picnic tables overlooking the sea and get some work done. It was sunny, as Mom had said, but it would move from chilly to cold once I got out of the harbor. I didn't want to go back to my apartment. Even though Chris was almost never there during the day, it would feel so empty I might not find the strength to leave. Instead, I went out to my Subaru and pulled my Snowden Family Clambake sweatshirt out of the back.

On my way to our Boston Whaler, which was tied up at the town pier, I stopped at our ticket kiosk to see if there were any more applications. There were three, a meager number but every little bit helped. Then I got in the Whaler and started her up. We had plenty of fuel. I headed into the harbor.

Morrow Island was empty when I got there. Empty of humans anyway. The construction at Windsholme was dormant while we awaited the arrival of the plumbers and electricians necessary for the next phase. Gulls screamed as I tied up the boat. A hawk circled looking for an unwary field mouse. On the dock, I stretched and took it all in—the little yellow house where I'd spent my childhood summers, and where my mother had spent hers, the dining pavilion where we served some of our guests, and the great lawn where we'd put out the bocce set and volley ball net when we opened in a week. I walked across the lawn on my way to the top of the island to Windsholme.

The mansion had been empty since the Depression, given just enough maintenance to keep it from falling down. Its central staircase had burned in a fire three years earlier, which had also put a hole in the roof. A year and a half before, my mother had come into some money and decided she would spend it fixing up the family home.

I had been against it, but slowly she'd convinced me we could use the ground floor for the business. Having enclosed, non-weather-dependent space would allow us to better support weddings and corporate retreats and the like, even run the clambake on iffy days. The upstairs would be converted to summer apartments, one for me and one for my mother. My sister and her family would remain in the little house down by the dock. Architects were found, and general contractors and teams of people had been coming and going, starting in early April when the weather allowed.

The house looked worse than ever. Back at the venture capital firm, when I'd worked with young companies suffering from growing pains, I often explained that things would get messier before they were fixed. "It's like cleaning out your closet," I told their management teams. "It always looks worse before it gets better." The executives would nod their agreement at my sage advice. But then again, I was representing the people who controlled their purse strings, so maybe they nodded to humor me.

All spring I had repeated the line about the closets whenever I saw Windsholme. The sagging front porch had been pulled off; its roof was held in place by two-by-fours angled into the ground. The shingle siding had been removed and replaced by horrible insulation wrap. Some of the windows were new, that was progress, and the hole in the roof was gone, but from the outside, the house looked naked and broken, shivering in her plastic blanket.

The workers had left a small stepladder propped against the threshold of the front door so they could get in and out. I climbed it, pushed the door open, and stepped into the hall.

The hole the fire had burned in the floor was gone; the scarred oak replaced by some kind of particle board that would be covered with hardwood later in the project. The ruined grand staircase was gone. There was a new stairway that followed the old contours in rough wood but without the original's elegant newel posts and banister, or any kind of bannister at all.

I stood in the big open space for a few moments, soaking it in. While the outside of the mansion looked worse than ever, inside there was progress. I climbed the new stairs, followed the hallway as it wound around the second floor and entered my apartment-to-be. The studs for the walls were up, awaiting the plumbers and electricians to do their work before they could be enclosed. I walked through the place, exploring my sitting room, bedroom, and office. It would be months before we got to make any of the fun decisions about cabinets and tile and appliances. Maybe not until next summer. But I could stand and look out the window that would be over my kitchen sink, down the rolling lawn and across the sea to the horizon.

And then I remembered. In my imagination, when I'd moved into this wonderful space, Chris had been by my side. He'd be incorporated into the world of the clambake, into my family, and we'd have island babies, like my mother and my sister had. Summoning the fantasy brought physical pain, a sharp stabbing in my chest that made it hurt to breathe.

All the fun of the tour of the house disappeared like a

popped balloon. Shoulders slumped, I made my way
downstairs and out the door, back into the bright sun-
shine.

I wasn't ready to leave Morrow Island, but the trip hadn't
had the settling effect Mom intended when she suggested it.
There was a steady breeze, something we treasured on
warm summer days, but today, it was too chilly to sit outside comfortably, the wind would cut through me. The
house by the dock was locked and I hadn't thought to
bring the key, so I headed for a picnic table in a corner of
the dining pavilion and hunkered down there.

I pulled the applications out of my tote bag and started
on the pile. I'd accidentally grabbed all of them, including the first four that I'd already rejected back at the
house. I quickly put them aside. The next applications I
looked at were the two people I'd already scheduled for
Sonny's interviews—Walter Hicks and Marty Flanagan.
Which reminded me, I was going to have to deal with
Sonny later. The picture of him hiding in my office like a
coward while she waited on the porch made my blood
boil.

The rest were unremarkable. There were some possible JOATS, servers, even one possibility for the crew of
the *Jacquie II*, the tour boat that carried our customers to
and from Morrow Island. I came, at last, to the three
forms I'd picked up in the kiosk that morning.

The first applicant from the new group looked fantastic for any number of positions. He had lot of restaurant
experience—waiter, cook, busboy, host. I scanned the
written application in wonder. How was this paragon still
looking for a seasonal gig? My eyes traveled down the
page. Mack Owen was listed as a reference. Interesting.
Then I went back to the top of the page. The application

was from Clark Kirwin. I couldn't believe it. But there it was in blue ballpoint pen. Clark Kirwin, The Chandlery, River Road, Damariscotta, Maine. I stared at it for a good long time. What was Clark up to? Ming had said Mack couldn't run the business without him.

Was Mack not giving him enough hours? It seemed doubtful. Mack was as strapped for help as we were. Lacey had applied to the clambake. Maybe she and Clark had some cozy notion about a romantic summer spent working on an island. They wouldn't be the first couple who had worked for us if they did.

As I stared, something else crept into focus. The handwriting. Clark's handwriting was strangely familiar . . .

I grabbed my phone. There was no service on the island, but the photo Andie had sent of the ransom note was still in the stored messages. The handwriting was identical. Or at least it appeared so to me. The letters were narrow and slanted bottom to top from left to right, which struck me as an unusual pattern. I examined the other applications for comparison, to make sure I wasn't seeing things. The more I stared, the more certain I was. I scooped up the papers, dumped them in the bag, and headed for the Whaler.

CHAPTER FIFTEEN

When the Whaler entered the harbor, my phone began to ding with text messages, voicemails, and emails that had arrived while I was out of range. Distracted boating is a thing, just like distracted driving, but I kept sneaking peeks at the phone, hoping for a message from Chris. There was none.

I tied up at the town pier and called the Damariscotta police station. The receptionist informed me that the detectives were far too busy to talk to me. I wondered if they were still with Mack or Ken Farrow but knew better than to ask. She said she would give them my message.

I went to Mom's and got my car. I thought about driving straight to Damariscotta to the police station, but I had no idea how long Binder and Flynn would be tied up, or whether information about a ransom note they considered to be a hoax would even interest them. I had Clark

Kirwin's phone number on his application, and I could have called him, but I didn't think it was a conversation for the phone. I definitely wasn't going to Pinney's house to find him since I'd been caught trespassing there twice already.

Instead, I took a chance, and went to Ocean View Motel.

The Ocean View was on a little hill right where downtown Busman's Harbor, with its Victorian houses and well-tended yards, met the two-lane highway that traveled up the peninsula to Route 1. It wasn't in a convenient, walkable in-town location, nor was it out by Route 1, which connected us to the rest of the midcoast. The motel was in a no-man's land, hospitality-industry-wise.

The Ocean View was a single-story building, a classic motor court from the olden days. Mustard-colored paint peeled off the stucco walls. The formerly white doors had old-fashioned keyed locks. The motel's single amenity, its sizable swimming pool, was still covered with a torn plastic cover.

It was easy to tell which unit must be Lacey's. While none of the rooms at the Ocean View had a view of the ocean, at least they looked out on the parking lot and pool. Except one room, which was wedged behind the motel office and accessed by a small covered passage. Its single window looked out on a mustard-colored wall three feet away from it. It would be the last room rented, the best room to barter for some overnight help. I raised my fist and knocked.

"Hello?" Lacey's voice was thin and tired. I could barely hear her through the door.

"Lacey, it's Julia Snowden. I'd like to talk to you."

"Julia?" The door creaked open and Lacey stood blinking at the sunlight. "Did you come to, you know, ask me more questions for the job interview?"

"No, I haven't. I came to ask you questions about Clark Kirwin."

Unless I was mistaken, Clark was her favorite subject. She wouldn't be able to resist. She looked back into the dark room. "Hold on. Let me put my shoes on. I'll come out."

When she came back, she was wearing black boots and the same oversized black sweater she'd worn to the interview. "We can go, like, over there." She led me across the parking lot and opened the gate to the chain-link fence around the pool. The outdoor furniture hadn't been put out, but there was a single round table and two chairs in one corner of the concrete apron. The table was a refuge for smokers, who presumably couldn't indulge in their rooms. A plastic ashtray overflowed with butts.

Lacey sat, and I did, too, ignoring the stench from the ashtray. "What about Clark?" she asked.

I realized, despite Lacey's apparent eagerness, I didn't have a way into this conversation. Much as she loved bragging about Clark, asking her directly, right off the bat, about the ransom note probably wouldn't get the result I wanted. I took the long way around.

"How did you and Clark meet?" I asked.

"We met this spring at Crowley's. I was with a girlfriend and he was by himself and we got to talking."

Crowley's opened in mid-April and it was pretty much the only place for people of legal drinking age to hang out in Busman's Harbor that early in the season. "Why was Clark in Busman's Harbor that night, did he say?"

"He hadn't been in Maine long," Lacey said. "I think he was checking out different places. He's a musician, you know. He wanted to see if Crowley's might be a place he could gig."

"I didn't know," I said. "I don't know much about Clark. I know he lives with his aunt and helps her out around the house. He works at Mack's Oyster Shack. His dad owns a place on Cape Cod. That's pretty much all I know. I'd like to know more. For example, what brought him to Maine?"

"He had a huge fight with his parents. He's taking a semester off from college to devote to his music. His parents are against it. His dad said if he wasn't going to school, he couldn't live with them. Clark spent the winter working at a restaurant near Sugarloaf. When the ski season ended, he came to Damariscotta to his aunt."

"Were they close, Clark and Pinney?"

"Not hardly. But they got close pretty quick. They have a lot in common."

"Like what?" *Beefs with Clark's father*, I imagined. I wasn't too far off the mark.

"Clark just fell in love with The Chandlery. Have you ever been there?"

"Pinney's house. Yes, I have."

"It's not exactly Pinney's house. It's part Clark's, too. Or it will be when his dad dies."

I put Pinney in her early sixties. She rowed six miles a day and didn't look to be kicking off any time soon. If Clark's dad was similar in age and fitness, Clark might have a long wait. Besides, how would that even work? Pinney shared ownership of the house with two brothers and three cousins. By the time it passed to all their progeny, there would be a dozen or more owners at least. Maine was littered with places like that, big old houses where there were so many owners, family members were

lucky to get a week in residence. And by three genera-
tions on, or five in the case of the Kirwins, the family
members were usually in quite different economic situa-
tions. Arguments about spending money for upkeep and
improvements were inevitable. Somebody always wanted
to extract whatever cash could be gotten. Take the money
and run. I seriously doubted Clark would be acting as the
lord of the manor at The Chandlery, unless he was a much
more talented musician than I suspected. Talented and
lucky to make enough money to buy his cousins and second cousins out.

"Clark and his aunt love The Chandlery," Lacey said.
"That made their relationship special. Clark's dad doesn't
love the place at all. Plus, Clark doesn't like the underhanded way his dad sold the oyster farm property out
from under his Aunt Pinney."

"Pinney told me she was out-voted by her co-owners."

"The house is in a trust. I don't understand exactly
how it works. But it didn't just happen, the others deciding to sell to Great River. Both times they sold, Clark's
dad went around to all the cousins and he was like, 'the
place is a dump. It's going to cost a fortune to fix it up.
Plus Pinney won't let any of us use it. We should sell part
of the land while we have the chance and fund some of
the maintenance of the remainder to protect our asset.'
And he got them all to sign. He called the house, 'our
asset.' That makes Clark so mad."

The Chandlery might need some work, but it wasn't a
dump. Windsholme had been a dump. I knew what a
dump looked like. "Pinney doesn't let the family use the
house?" I asked. How could that be?

"Of course she *would* let them use it. It's just that they
only want to come at inconvenient times." Unconsciously,

Lacey did such a dead-on impression of Pinney Kirwin I almost laughed out loud. It was time to move the conversation along. "Was Clark opposed to Andie's lease expansion the way Pinney was?"

"He hated it! It made him so mad. It's bad enough having that fish farm next door, no way were they going to allow it to get bigger."

Pinney had called Great River a fish farm. Her influence on Lacey was strong, though I couldn't tell if it was directly or via Clark. "Lacey, why did you go to work for Andie Greatorex if Clark and his aunt hated the farm so much?"

"That was Clark's idea. He thought I could spy on Andie. But it didn't work out. I wasn't comfortable. When I agreed to do it, I didn't know her. But then, after she interviewed me and spent a couple hours on my first day training me, I liked her. I told Clark I couldn't go through with it."

If Lacey liked Andie, what had been behind the scene I'd witnessed at the store? "So then you collected your pay and quit?" I prompted.

"Not exactly." Lacey chewed her lower lip. "I quit, but I forgot to tell her I quit. I felt so bad about the whole thing I never wanted to see her again. But then Clark kept at me. He told me Andie absolutely owed me the money and I had to go get it. I didn't want to, and we got into a huge fight. He drove me there and we were yelling the whole time and then I got out of his car and slammed the door and went and got my check because I wasn't going to listen to him one minute more." She was breathing rapidly when she finished the story.

"Lacey." When I had her attention, I put my phone with the photo of the ransom note and Clark's application

on the table. "Did Clark steal Andie's Greatorex's oyster
spat and then try to get her to pay ransom for it?"

"No! He never stole anything." And then she burst into
tears. "But he warned me people might say he had," she
choked out. She sobbed for a while, wiping her nose on
the long sleeve of the black sweater. She was crying way
beyond what the simple denial about the robbery called
for. They were tears that had been coming for a long time.

Finally, she hiccupped to a stop and I judged it was
okay to press her again. "If Clark didn't steal the seed,
and I absolutely believe you," I assured her, though I absolutely did not, "then did he write this ransom note, because the handwriting looks exactly the same to me."

Exactly the same was a bit of an exaggeration. It wasn't
like I could do a word-for-word comparison. But Lacey
bought it.

"It was a joke!" I thought she might go into hysterics
again, but she pulled it together. "We did it together, as a
joke. Clark thought it was so funny. Who would kidnap
baby oysters? We were at Clark's house hanging out. We
started making up stories about kidnappings and ransom
notes and teeny, tiny heiresses dressed in high heels and
tiaras. We were laughing so hard I practically peed myself, and then we just wrote the note. We made it up together, but he wrote it down."

"And you left it under Andie's cottage door?" I was
sure they had been in Crowley's when Andie received the
note. Had they placed it there earlier and Andie had
missed it?

"We *didn't*. We didn't deliver the note to her house. It
would be rude and scary to get the note at your house at
night. We taped it to the door of the shop. She was meant
to understand it was a *joke*."

"Andie found it at her cottage. It was delivered when she went to pick up take-out."

"We left it on the shop door, I swear. She must have told you the wrong place."

But she hadn't. I was certain. Who had found the note at the shop and delivered it to Andie? "You talked to the police," I said. "Did you tell them about writing the note as a joke and leaving it at the shop?"

"No." Lacey pulled herself into her sweater as if she wanted to disappear. "Clark said we should say we didn't know anything and that's what I did, even though that cop with the short hair scared me. But Clark and me, we stick together."

I tried to work out how telling me wasn't a violation of their pact, but I wasn't law enforcement and Lacey was stressed to the max. She needed to tell someone. In spite of myself, I felt sorry for her.

"If you and Clark didn't move the note, who do you think did?"

"I think it was that creepy guy who kept hanging around the shop. He scared me."

Creepy guy? "Did you not like Josh?"

"Josh is fine. I only met him for like, two minutes. I was hired mostly to work when Josh wasn't there. No. I mean that old guy, Mr. Farrow, with the white hair and the black eyebrows. He kept coming by."

Ken Farrow. Hanging around the Great River shop. He could easily have found the ransom note and delivered it to Andie. "Did you tell Clark you thought Mr. Farrow delivered the note?"

"Yes. At first, he didn't agree with me. He likes Mr. Farrow. But lately he's been saying maybe it was him."

"What about Pinney? Could she have found the note?"

Lacey shook her head. "Ms. Kirwin never went *near* Great River. Ever. She hates that place."

"I'd like to talk to Clark about all this," I said. "To clear the air." I was going to talk to him whatever she said.

"Will he get in trouble?"

"I'm not a lawyer, but I don't think you can get in trouble for writing a note for a ransom that never got paid." Of course you could, but Lacey didn't question me. She was a trusting soul.

"As a *joke*," she insisted again.

"Do you know where Clark is?"

"He's at his house." She must have sensed my hesitation. "He goes to work at Mack's in about an hour," she added.

"Thanks. I'll catch him there."

I made it to Damariscotta in thirty minutes. It's way too easy to speed on the back roads, especially in the off-season when traffic is light. I wasn't sure if Lacey would call Clark the moment I left the motel to tell him that she'd confessed their involvement with the ransom note to me. I didn't think she would. She was clearly intimidated by Clark and she wouldn't want to tell him what she'd done, even though he was inevitably going to find out. She'd gamble he'd take his anger out on me, rather than yelling at her. She'd do anything to avoid that.

Of course the ransom note was meant as a joke. It read like a joke. But whoever had pushed it under Andie's door during the specific window when she was away from the cottage hadn't meant it as a joke. It was meant to intimidate.

Lacey thought it was Ken Farrow. It made sense to me what she said about Pinney never going over to the Great River shop. But that didn't mean she hadn't heard Clark and Lacey joking around about the note and gone there on purpose to retrieve it. Still, I thought Farrow was a good bet.

I went straight to the police station. The receptionist informed me stiffly that the detectives were "tied up with important things." I assumed those "important things" were Mack Owen and Ken Farrow being questioned about their suspicious conversation the night before. I left messages for Binder and Flynn to call me and moved on.

I had time to kill before Clark would show up at Mack's. I was trying to work out how and why Ken Farrow might have moved the "joke" ransom note. Josh had said Farrow was always hanging around Great River. Finding the ransom note would have been easy enough, but how had he known exactly when Andie would be out in order to deliver it? Had he hidden on the farm property, waiting for her to leave? It seemed unlikely. His boat or his car would be visible, and he wouldn't want that. And she might have never gone out that night.

I drove to Midden Bay, gambling I was correct that Ken was still at the police station. When I parked by the house, Red gave out a couple of dispirited "woofs," from the inside like he'd lost interest in being a guard dog a long time ago but was still on the payroll and had to make a minimal effort. "Good boy," I called out to him and walked down the lawn to Ken's dock. The river wasn't busy, nothing like it would be at peak summer, but the sounds of grunts and bangs, swearing and mechanical noises echoed around as boats went in the water. From time to time, the buzz of a small outboard motor, the kind you'd use on a dinghy, filled the air.

Across the river, I could see Andie's bright red pickup clearly where it was parked by her cottage. It would have been well into dusk when the ransom note was delivered to Andie. At first, I thought that would make it harder to see the red truck leave its spot and bump along the dirt road from the cottage to the farm road. But then I realized Andie would have put on her headlights, which would have made seeing the truck easier, not harder. I remembered Farrow telling me he'd watched the activity at Andie's farm on the day of the murder through his binoculars. Bingo. He could definitely have seen Andie leave that night.

So the question was, could Farrow have made it from his farm to Andie's cottage, and slipped the ransom note under her door in the half hour she said she was out?

I jogged back to the Subaru, waving to Red whose head appeared in the front window as I went by. I drove to Andie's front door with ten minutes to spare.

Farrow was against Andie's lease expansion. Farrow thought he and Mack would have a deal if Andie was intimidated into withdrawing her application. My only question was, had Farrow extended his campaign of harassment to murder?

Ming was at the bar at Mack's Shack when I walked in, giving the bartender with the ponytail instructions. I sat at the bar a few stools away from them, not interrupting exactly, but close enough that Ming would notice me.

She came over as soon as her conversation was done. "Hi, Julia. What brings you here?"

"I was hoping to talk to Clark Kirwin, actually."

She looked exasperated, like she had more than enough on her plate without having to track down employees for me. "I don't think he's in yet."

"I can wait." I was sorely tempted to order a cocktail, but I had to keep my wits about me.

"Suit yourself." But then the haughty features softened. "I'm sorry." She sat on the stool next to me. "I'm tense. Mack's been at the police station for six hours. I can't imagine what's happening."

"Has he been arrested?"

"Not that I've heard. I'm sure he would have called me." Her face collapsed into a frown. "Do you think he will be?"

"No, of course not."

"I know it looks bad that he's the heir and the farm and property are worth so much. And the insurance. He and Andie set it up that way back when they were partners. I'm sure Andie thought she had plenty of time to change it. Mack changed his when we got married. I guess Andie never had an incentive."

"I know Lieutenant Binder and Sergeant Flynn," I said. "They're careful. They follow the investigation and don't jump to conclusions." *Though if they heard two people talking about a possible conspiracy to harm the victim that didn't help.* I kept that thought to myself.

I pulled my cell phone out of my tote bag and put it on the bar. I told myself I was checking the time, but of course I stole a glance to see if Chris had called. There was nothing. I was shocked to discover I hadn't checked in over an hour.

Ming saw me look. "Do you need to be somewhere?" She sounded hopeful.

"No, just checking for messages."

She got down from her stool. She was short enough it involved a little hop. "I'll send Clark to you as soon as he arrives." She ducked her head and her dark hair fell around her face. "I'm really sorry if I caused any trouble last night." When I didn't say anything, she went on. "Between you and Chris, I mean. I realized later; I shouldn't have said what I did about inviting you to couples' night. I was embarrassed and afraid you'd think we were unfriendly. I should have equally realized it was possible you didn't want to come."

"I would have loved to have come." The words were out of my mouth before I thought them through.

Ming looked startled, though whether it was at the content or intensity of my answer I couldn't tell. "Why didn't you?"

Ah, here was the rub. "Because Chris didn't invite me." I wasn't sure I wanted to admit something like this to a relative stranger, but in my determination not to discuss what was happening with my mother or sister, I was left with no one to talk to.

Ming's mouth dropped open and she gave a little, very little, feminine snort of surprise. "I didn't know. I wouldn't have guessed. Is he ashamed of us?"

"He loves you guys," I answered. "I've never gotten the impression ever that he was ashamed of you." I stopped, wondering if I should give voice to the feeling that had been churning my guts since the night before. "I think he's ashamed of me."

"Not possible." Ming put her hand on my forearm. "He brags about you all the time. I've never seen him talk about any woman the way he talks about you." When I didn't say anything, she went on. "If Chris isn't ashamed of us, and he isn't ashamed of you, I think, on some level, he must be ashamed of himself. Deep down, there's a reason he can't be comfortable with who he is."

CHAPTER SIXTEEN

At a quarter to five, Mack came into the restaurant, shoulders hunched, face drawn. He didn't look right or left and certainly didn't see me by the bar. He trooped dejectedly toward his office.

Clark showed up a few minutes later. The drinkers and early diners were drifting in. The waitstaff had kept up with the tables, there wasn't much cleanup to be done. He could spare time for me.

"Ming says you wanted to talk to me."

I glanced at the bartender. She was occupied with two people who'd sat on the other side of the bar, but I didn't think she would stay that way. "Let's sit in a booth," I said to Clark.

"Ming didn't exactly give me permission to sit out here." He glanced around, uneasy.

He was dressed in his blue Mack's Shack jacket, ready

for duty. Mack's wasn't a place with formal service and rules about the help fraternizing with the guests. "She gave me permission," I said. "Let's go over here."

I led him across the room to a booth. The restaurant was still pretty empty. There was no one in the booths on either side of us.

Clark sat down, put his elbows on the table and looked at me. He was edgy and hostile, but also curious. Obviously, Lacey hadn't called him.

"I spoke to Lacey today," I started.

He pursed his mouth. He was perplexed but not hostile. "Is she going to get that job at your place?"

"We didn't talk about the job. We talked about you. Clark, there's no easy way to put this. I noticed the handwriting on your application for a job at the clambake is the same as the handwriting on the ransom note for Andie Greatorex's oyster spat. Lacey confirmed you two wrote the ransom note."

His first instinct was denial. Big, broad denial. He slapped a hand on the table so hard the silverware jumped, and then shouted "No!" loudly enough that people turned from across the room. He realized he was attracting unwanted attention and lowered his voice. "I never did that."

As I had with Lacey, I placed my phone on the table open to the photo of the note and then put the application next to it. "Even if Lacey hadn't confessed," I said, "I have all the proof I need. I'm taking these to the police as soon as I leave here."

He didn't think to ask how I came to have a photo of the note. "I didn't write that note." He was a master of the bald-faced lie. "And even if I did, why tell me about it? Why not take it to the police."

"It will be better if you go to the police and tell them

Barbara Ross

what you did," I said. "I wanted to give you, and Lacey, that chance."

"I don't see why we would." But even as he said it, some of the facade was crumbling. He squirmed on the banquette, unable to get comfortable, physically or emotionally.

"Because you're in big trouble," I said. "Really big trouble. Your ransom note is so amateurish, the state police and the local police have assumed it was a hoax, that the person who wrote it didn't steal Andie's oyster seed. But when the state police detectives question you about this, I think they'll figure it wasn't a hoax. Not really. Because you're the one who stole the seed."

He'd looked dejected when I started and by the end of my speech all the fight had gone out of him. He sat in the booth, mouth opening and closing like a beached fish, and then he cried. He cupped his hands around his face, hiding his tears from his co-workers and customers.

I hadn't been surprised in the least by Lacey's tears, but I was flabbergasted by Clark's. He had seemed so full of himself, so full of bravado. But as he sobbed silently, I could see that the events of the last several days, and his part in them, had been putting more weight on his shoulders than he was able to carry.

"I didn't kill her," he croaked when he was finally able to speak.

He looked genuinely miserable. Not scared because he was guilty, but scared he had, through his own stupidity, gotten himself into a situation that could send him to prison for the rest of his life. He was terrified.

"That's why you need to go to the police," I said. "Tell them what you've done before they figure it out. And tell them what you haven't done, before they reach their own conclusion."

"It was so stupid. The robbery was meant to scare her. She wasn't supposed to get hurt." He closed his eyes and steepled his hands over his nose, holding back more tears. "I was supposed to grab the buckets and run. I figured I was bigger. I had the element of surprise. But she was so strong. She held on to the pails with all her might. I couldn't run away empty-handed. I shoved her and kicked her. It wasn't supposed to have happened." He gulped and I thought for a moment he might be sick. "But I didn't kill her. I swear. I almost had a heart attack when I heard she was dead. That's when I told Lacey to lie. I knew if we told the truth about the ransom note, they police would figure out about the robbery and the cops would automatically assume I killed her."

"That's why you need to tell them the full story. Yourself, voluntarily." I shifted on the banquette to sit up as high as I could. He was a lot taller than me and I wanted to look him in the eye. "Andie had the idea the person who robbed her was paid to do it by someone else. Did someone pay you, Clark?"

He looked relieved that I'd asked him the direct question, even as he denied it. "No one paid me," he said quietly.

"Then what? There's something you're not telling me about how this went down." I sat there stubbornly, like I was willing to sit forever.

It turned out it wasn't necessary. Clark was dying to tell someone his secret. He'd been keeping it for too long. "Nobody paid me. But someone suggested I should do it. And told me the time of the delivery. And he egged me on." Clark was aggrieved, like he was the injured party and not the perpetrator.

"Who? Who egged you on?" I asked him.

"Ken Farrow," he answered. "It was all his idea. I gave him the spat after I did it."

I called ahead to Flynn, who finally picked up, to make sure he and Binder were still at the police station. "Wait there," I told him, "I'm bringing someone along who needs to talk to you."

"Righto," Flynn said, not asking any questions.

Clark and I agreed it would be better if he left his car at Mack's and I drove him. He was shaky and alternately tearful and angry, but most of all I wanted to make sure he went inside. His only ties to the area were his aunt and Lacey and it was easy to picture him driving past the station and on out of town. When we got there, I left the car and walked him in. I could tell he was having second thoughts by the hesitation in his step, but he'd confessed to me, he was at the police station, so there was nothing to do but go through with it.

The receptionist was gone, but Flynn was waiting in the lobby area. "All yours," I said. "Clark, good luck."

I didn't want to drive all the way back to Busman's Harbor. I was tense and on edge. Things were happening. Things were going to happen. I went back to the bar at Mack's to wait.

The restaurant had filled steadily as I sat with Clark, and by the time I returned it was hopping. I found a stool on the corner on the far side of the bar with a good view of the front door. Mercifully, there was no one next to me.

No need to make conversation. A second bartender, a guy, had come on to help the young woman bartender. He seemed focused on filling the drink orders the servers dropped off and picked up, while she waited on the bar customers.

"Back so soon?" She smiled at me. "That was quite a conversation you were having with Clark over there in the booth."

We must have been the talk of the restaurant. He was supposed to be on shift, and we'd walked out with no explanation. I ordered a glass of Malbec and smiled back.

Ming looked frantically busy. She whipped around the floor, checking in with servers, customers, and the hostess. I studied her, professional to professional. At the Snowden Family Clambake, it was my job to make sure everything ran smoothly. At times it felt like spinning plates. Ming was good at it.

When she came to check on the bar, she stopped next to me. "Are you okay?" she asked.

"I could ask you the same."

"I'm fine," she said. "The police only wanted to speak to Mack as a witness. I sent him home. I told him to keep the sitter there and go straight to bed. He was exhausted. Now I'm doing the best I can, though it's taking time to get my rhythm back. I didn't expect to take over so soon."

Ming left and the bartender brought my wine. I settled in for what might be a long wait. I wasn't clear on what Binder and Flynn would do. I assumed they would arrest Clark if he went through with it and confessed to the assault and robbery. If he were arrested, he'd be bailed out if his Aunt Pinney had anything to say about it. And then, if Clark went through with it and implicated Ken Farrow, Binder and Flynn would bring Farrow back in for another chat.

But then, in the moment I thought about him, Ken Farrow walked into the restaurant. He didn't have the same defeated posture after his all-day interrogation as Mack had. Farrow walked with a certain swagger, or maybe it was a sway. I couldn't be sure. I wondered if he would lose the bravado if he knew what Clark Kirwin was telling Binder and Flynn at that very moment.

Farrow spotted the empty stool next to me and came over. "Ms. Snowden, mind if I join you?"

What was I supposed to say to that? It was a public accommodation. Like every woman who has ever sat at a bar, I had perfected an icy stare. I turned it on him, with no apparent effect.

"I couldn't sit at home," he muttered. "Whisky and soda," he said to the bartender. When she tried to ask if he had a preferred whiskey, he waved her away.

I could tell by the smell of him the drink he'd ordered wasn't his first. He'd probably been drinking since he'd been released from the police station. I didn't think he should have driven to the restaurant, but he probably had.

I turned my back to him and pulled out my phone. **Farrow at Mack's**, I typed to Flynn. I slid my phone back in my tote and faced the bar. I didn't think Farrow had seen.

Farrow didn't say anything to me until after he was served. I stared ahead, sipping my wine. "Spent all day with the cops," he said, by way of an opener.

I didn't respond.

"Your aunt and uncle seem to think I put Andie's oyster spat pails in their shed. They *allege* it," he emphasized, spraying me with spittle.

"Did you?"

The question brought him up short. He hadn't expected me to be that direct. He leaned so far away from me on his stool I thought he might fall over. But then he shocked me by responding. "Why would I do that?"

"Because Clark Kirwin told me you talked him into stealing the seed and he gave the pails and the spat to you."

Farrow was surprised, but not knocked off his game. "I told you. I've got no upwellers."

"I don't know where the seed went," I said. "But you put the pails in my uncle's shed." I waited until the bartender, who'd been wiping the sleek, dark wood of the bar, walked away. "*And,* I think you found the joke ransom note Clark and Lacey Brenneman wrote and you delivered it to Andie's cottage."

"What?" His black eyebrows, those hairy caterpillars, flew up practically to his hairline. "I never did that. And before you even say it, I didn't kill her, either."

"From where I sit, it doesn't look good for you."

"Really, young lady. You have no idea what you're talking about. I've got an ace in the hole. An ace in the hole," he repeated.

I was impressed by his confidence, so unlike Lacey and Clark who'd come undone. But he was older and wilier. "What is this ace?" I asked.

"Something I'm saving in case the cops arrest me. If I told you, it wouldn't be in the hole, would it? I know you're friendly with those detectives. Everybody in town knows it."

"Suit yourself." I finished my wine and considered ordering another.

A wave of conversation rippled through the restaurant.

Voices got louder; tones more vehement. Lieutenant Binder and Sergeant Flynn had arrived. They turned, surveying the room. Binder spotted Farrow sitting next to me and they hustled over.

"Kenneth Farrow, it appears our business isn't over for the day. We need you to come with us," Binder said.

"Am I under arrest?" He had been briefly knocked back when Binder and Flynn had entered the restaurant. I could tell by his sharp intake of breath. But his confidence returned quickly.

"We're not arresting you, no," Binder answered. "But if you decline to come with us, I'm happy to go to a judge and get a warrant."

"Okay, okay." He slid off the stool, swaying a little when his feet hit the floor. He turned to me. "Can you please go feed Red? And make sure he gets out. He'll be dancing a jig right about now."

As Binder and Flynn walked him out the door, Farrow turned and threw me his keys. I caught them one-handed. Farrow cocked an eyebrow at me.

"Can I?" I shouted at Binder and Flynn's retreating backs, but everyone in the restaurant was talking at once and neither of them heard me.

CHAPTER SEVENTEEN

I sat at the bar for almost a half an hour. It took a long time for the restaurant to settle down. I watched as Ming Owen circulated, visiting many of the tables, asking about weather and fish and grandchildren. Anything to change the subject.

Finally, I couldn't stand it any longer.

Farrow's green pickup with MIDDEN BAY OYSTER FARM stenciled on the side was still in Mack's parking lot. I got in the Subaru and drove to Farrow's farm.

I parked out front in the little dirt lot I used when I first visited the farm. As I came up on the porch, I could see Red through the big window in the front door. He gave a little tail wave and a "woof."

"It's okay boy, I'm here." I figured out which key went into the lock pretty easily. It was the one that looked as old as the door. The lock didn't stick, which surprised me given its age. I pushed the door open and was inside.

The light switch was to the left of the door, a panel of three, and I flipped them all on—porch light, hallway light, and the light at the top of the stairs. Red had already run eagerly to the kitchen and I followed him, turning lights on as I went. He stood over his stainless-steel bowl looking up at me with round brown, cloudy eyes.

The was a quarter of a bottle of Jameson's on the table and an empty glass.

"I know you're hungry," I told the dog, "but I think we'd better go outside first." There was a leash hanging by the kitchen door. I knew he went out on the property without one. I'd seen him with Farrow more than once, but I didn't trust my ability to command him. He sat and watched without objecting as I fastened the leash to his collar.

Outside, I kept us in the circle cast by the porch light. Over the river, the stars were bright. Andie's cottage was dark, of course, but lights shone from the ground floor of Pinney's windows. I wondered if she'd gotten the call that Clark was at the police station.

Red did what he needed to and pulled me back toward the house, anxious for his dinner. I located some cans in a cupboard and a can opener in a drawer and dumped the smelly food into his bowl. He lunged for it and almost swallowed it whole. "It's okay, boy," I said.

I got ready to go; mission accomplished. If Farrow were arrested and held overnight, I'd come back in the morning until provisions were made for Red. I assumed there would be a search of the place, if there hadn't been already. The house wasn't the crime scene, that was on the river bottom. But he might have dumped the seed out somewhere on the property.

Which reminded me what Farrow had said. He'd taken the plans for the expansion of Great River from Andie's desk. Maybe that was his ace in the hole.

The long, plastic-topped folding table Farrow used as a desk was in the living room against the back wall. It was covered in papers—invoices for equipment like cages, buoys, and lines to be used on the farm, fuel for his boat and repairs for the outboard. I shuffled the papers around, looking for Andie's plan. The cops had been through Andie's desk. The plan couldn't have meant too much to them. Under all the stuff was a large piece of paper. It had been loosely folded, not creased. Gingerly, I picked it out of the pile and opened it.

I had found it, the plan for the extended dock system at Great River. I hadn't put a light on in the living room, so I took it out to the hallway for a better look. What I saw wasn't surprising, nothing more than what a larger operation would require. A second sorting shed, more dock space and floats for the upwellers, more space for small boats. It didn't seem like a big deal. Anyone could have figured out that if Andie got the lease expansion, she'd need to expand her operation on land, too.

The drawings had no markings on them to indicate they'd been filed with any authority or any permits had been applied for. Since we were building on waterfront property at Windsholme, I knew there were months, possibly years of work with the town, state, and federal governments to get the necessary permissions even to begin. This was Andie, looking ahead, hoping to get the lease expansion. It was not an immediate threat to anyone. I could see why the cops had left it. It wasn't Farrow's ace in the hole.

It was hard to look at the whole big plan while I was holding it. I took it into the kitchen, turned on the over-head light, moved the Jameson's bottle and the glass to the drainboard, and spread out the plan on the kitchen table. Something bothered me about it.

When I looked more carefully, I realized that on the slope above the second dock was a second shipping barn, a new building. And above that was a dedicated tasting room, replacing the picnic tables with a screened gazebo where customers could eat their oysters. I stared at it until I finally realized what I was looking at.

The Great River Oyster Farm property had doubled in size because the plan included all of the Kirwin property. The Chandlery was gone, and the oyster farm now ex-tended across the riverfront. It was as large as Kirwin's original shipyard had been.

How was that going to happen?

I picked the plan up and started to refold it. The weight of the paper was odd. I couldn't get it back the way it had been. I turned the big sheet over. Something was taped to the back of it, a piece of eight by ten white printer paper. There was writing on the other side. Slowly, I peeled the tape off.

It was a simple document, written in courier font, its round letters imitating a typewriter's. In concise, formal language the document stated, "We the beneficiaries of the Kirwin Family Trust direct the trustees to offer the house and property known The Chandlery, the only re-maining asset of the trust, for sale, and to sell it to the highest acceptable bidder."

It was dated three weeks earlier and signed by three

men with the surname Kirwin, and two women, one named Taylor and one Robinson. Pinney's brothers and cousins, I assumed. There was a blank line above the typed name "Penelope Kirwin."

My heart beat so hard I felt a little faint. Pinney's relatives were not only eager to sell The Chandlery, they were willing to see it torn down.

I texted Flynn. **At Farrow house. Something you need to see.** He and Binder would be furious I'd been there. I'd have to deal with their anger sometime, it was a question of when. They were undoubtedly busy with Farrow and neither one of them would be looking at their texts. I pressed on the tape to stick the document to the back of the plan and put it back on the plastic folding table where I'd found it. I walked through the house, turning out the lights. At the door I gave Red a good-bye pet. I decided to leave the porch light on. I had no desire to walk out into the dark.

On the porch, the door locked as easily as it had unlocked. Red was visible in the glow the porch light threw back into the hallway. He gave me one more forlorn look and I waved to him through the window in the door as I backed away, until I was almost to the steps.

His face changed, he showed his teeth and emitted a low growl. "I know boy. I'm sorry," I said. And then everything went black.

I awoke in darkness. I was on the floor, lying on my right side. I reached for my phone and discovered my hands were tied together behind my back. I was alone, at least for the moment. I quieted my breathing and listened.

From not far away came the sound of water lapping

against rocks. A boat creaked as the water moved it against a wooden dock, and then away, and then back again. The Damariscotta River. I would have bet my life on it. I quite possibly had.

I leaned slightly and lay my cheek on the floor. It was wood. Rough and dirty. My legs weren't tied. I kicked out and immediately struck something hard with a metallic sound that ponged through the space. I tried again and succeeded in turning myself slightly. I searched for light seeping in from somewhere, but everything was the same inky black.

I was in a shed by the water. Ken Farrow's sorting and storage shed, I guessed. I remembered it had a window. I tried again to get oriented, hoping for a glimpse of stars. If I was in his shed, I was too far from the house for the porch light to reach. Not that Farrow would have left it on after he bashed me.

I lay there, breathing heavily, trying to work out what had happened. Binder and Flynn must have finished with Farrow much sooner than I'd anticipated. Had they not believed Clark Kirwin at all? Maybe Clark was their suspect and they were checking details with Farrow, instead of the other way around. Or something . . . I racked my brain.

Red had growled before I'd been hit. If it had been his owner behind me, he would have wagged his tail and maybe whined at Ken to hurry up and come inside. It had been a stranger who'd hit me. A stranger to Red, if not to me.

I shivered. It was cold and the arm I lay on was asleep. Without using my tied hands, could I lever myself to standing? I curled up, stuck out my left leg and tried to use it to push myself to my knees, but the physics were all wrong. I didn't know when the person who'd done this to me would be back. I flailed noisily for a second, then thought better of it. I didn't know if he was close by, standing guard.

I started again, slowly inching forward like a sideways worm. I hadn't gone far when my cheek hit metal and there was a terrible crash as something heavy fell across my body. I yelped and shook it off, forgetting my vow to be quiet. It clattered to the floor beside me. From the weight of the handle, I was sure it was some kind of heavy gardening implement, a pitchfork, or a spade. What moving it did achieve, aside from adding an extra jolt of adrenaline to my overloaded body, was to clear a space by a wall. I raised my head and rested the side of my forehead against it. The rough wood confirmed it. I was in a shed.

I took a deep breath and flipped onto my back. It meant my tied arms were pinned underneath me, which made me feel like a helpless turtle on its shell, but I could use the heels of my boots to push, and slowly, inch by agonizing inch, I was sitting with my back against the wall.

It dawned me slowly, now that I had my bearings, that the space I was in was even smaller than Ken Farrow's shed. For one thing, as my eyes adjusted to the dark, I was certain there was no window. I leaned to my left and came up against something I judged to be a lawn rake by the way it tensed and then sprung back when I leaned on the handle. To my right were two round wooden poles. I couldn't figure out what they were.

It was likely as I pushed myself up, I would knock the rake on my right or the things on my left over, maybe both, creating a racket. But I had to try. I would be safer standing. I pulled my feet under me and pressed up, leaning against the wall. My useless, tied hands dragged against the rough wood. I could feel the splinters as they entered my skin.

At last, breathless, I was on my feet, slightly dizzy, but determined to find the door. I leaned to my right and felt the implements next to me against my cheek. They were smooth, curved. They were oars.

I was in Pinney Kirwin's shed. I was sure of it.

Because Ken Farrow hadn't killed Andie. He'd stalked her, harassed her, taken advantage of her friendship. But he hadn't killed her. Pinney had.

The footsteps outside were so soft I almost didn't hear them over my own labored breathing. But then I did. What if it wasn't Pinney but someone who could help me? I stood still, pulse beating in my throat. If it was Pinney, she didn't know I was conscious. She didn't know I was standing. It was too much of an advantage to gamble away.

I didn't know where I was in the shed relative to the door. I was confident I wasn't leaning against it. My plan was when she opened it to hurl myself at her the moment I figured out where she was.

But she didn't come. I turned my ear to the wall and listened. The footsteps continued. She even hummed a little. I heard a slash, like water in a metal container, and the thwap of liquid as it hit the ground.

Then I smelled it. Gasoline.

I had to get out. I edged along the wall, smelling for the air that would come in around the door to tell me where it was. I was terrified of knocking something over and I shuffled cautiously but steadily, as if my feet were bound as well as my hands. I found the spot where the smell of gas was overwhelming. I was at the door.

I pressed cautiously. It gave a little but didn't move. I hadn't expected it to. I leaned all my weight against it. I felt the door bow at the center but it didn't give. It was a flimsy wooden door. A shed door. I could take it.

There was nothing to be done but to take a run at it. I stepped back carefully. There was a whoosh outside as the flames started. I ran, shoulder to the door. I smacked it so hard it took my breath away, but then it blasted open.

With my hands behind my back my balance was already compromised, and I staggered forward. It took a second to adjust to the greater amount of light. The lights shining from the windows of The Chandlery showed Pinney Kirwin walking away, her dirty work done for the night.

A faint sound of sirens gave me hope. I would head toward them wherever they were. But the river distorted the sound and when I dared to look behind me, the police cars were on the other side, roaring onto Ken Farrow's property.

The sound caused Pinney to turn, too, and she saw me in the firelight. Her mouth flew open and she came at me at a run. I took off toward Andie's cottage.

In the woods, the ambient light from The Chandlery dimmed to nonexistent. Because they were bound, I couldn't put my hands in front of me to soften the blow from a trunk or a branch. If I tripped, I couldn't break my fall. At first, it made me timid and I trotted, but then I heard Pinney gaining on me. I was younger, but her legs and cardiovascular system had been made strong by her daily rowing, so I put my head down and ran for the farm road. Once I was on it, I could find my way to the streetlights on the River Road. If I fell, I wouldn't make it. If she caught me, I wouldn't make it.

When I got to Andie's cottage, I could see her driveway. I ran down it full tilt. It was uneven and sloped toward the sides, but there weren't any trees. When I reached the farm road, I headed for the River Road. Behind me, Pinney was finally beginning to lag.

And then, down on the road, there were sirens and lights, and then door slams and voices. "I'm here! I'm here," I screamed, but I was so out of breath my voice had no power.

Flynn was by the unmarked car. I don't know what attracted his attention—my movement, my footsteps, or the sound of my ragged breathing. He ran toward me and caught me in his arms. "Whoa! Julia, slow down."

"She's right behind me." I wheezed the words out. Then I turned. She was gone.

The sound of an enormous explosion rocketed through the night.

CHAPTER EIGHTEEN

The same EMT I'd had the last time sat with me in the back of the ambulance while the police went after Pinney Kirwin. They left one young state trooper behind to take photos of my bound arms before he cut me loose.

The EMT checked me out. "What hurts?" she asked, surveying me.

"My shoulder." It hadn't hurt so much when I'd been running, but the minute my hand had been unbound and my shoulder could move back to its normal position it began radiating pain. "Ouch," I said when she moved my arm. "And my head hurts."

"For what it's worth, I don't think your shoulder is broken. But a blow to the head could be serious. You're going to the hospital this time."

"I'm not that uncomfortable," I said. "I'd like to wait until the detectives get back."

Half an hour later, Flynn came back alone.

"Did you get her?" I asked.

"We did. She fought like a hellcat. She barricaded herself in the house."

"She was never leaving the house," I told him. "That was the point."

"You're going to the ER now," he said. "We'll talk more in the morning."

"I don't have my cell phone. I think Pinney took it."

Flynn pulled his out of his jacket. "Do you want me to call Chris?" he asked.

I hesitated for a moment. "Call my mom."

Binder and Flynn arrived in my room at Busman's Harbor Hospital at the same time as my breakfast tray. I had finally persuaded Mom to go home and get some sleep.

I was achy all over, much worse than I'd expected. I had cuts and scrapes that burned despite the painkillers.

"Were they all in it together—Farrow, Clark, and Pinney?" I asked.

"Yes, and no," Binder said. "Farrow convinced Clark to pull off the robbery. Clark already had a simmering sense of injustice that his father, I gather there are some issues there, had sold his birthright, the part of the estate that had already gone to Great River. Why he thought the property was his birthright is unclear. There are a dozen heirs in his generation. But Pinney, seeing an ally in Clark, had fanned the flames, and from there Farrow had only to suggest the robbery."

"And Ken wanted Andie robbed because—"

"He believed it was paramount for her to withdraw her

lease application. He'd seen the handwriting on the wall. The lease was going to be granted. The only way to prevent it was to carry on a campaign of harassment. He started small with her cages and buoys. The point was to make her uneasy so when the coup de grace came, the robbery, she'd already be off balance. He believed the robbery would freak her out to the point she'd drop the application."

"He didn't know Andie well if he thought that would work," I said.

"She was young. She was a woman," Binder said. "He thought Andie had been less instrumental in building the business than Mack. But he did come to understand she didn't scare easily. That's why he moved from harassment to robbery.

"Farrow didn't want to be recognized, which is why he solicited Clark Kirwin to commit the actual crime," Binder continued. "He met Clark at Mack's shortly after he got to town. Farrow recognized the name and got close to him, hanging around the restaurant late at night for extended conversations."

"The robbery was a mess," Flynn said. "Kirwin wasn't supposed to hurt her for one thing. And he was supposed to yell, 'Drop the lease!' or some such, so Ms. Greatorex would know why she was being attacked. It was a campaign of intimidation."

"She figured out the reason for the attack," I said. "She simply wasn't easily intimidated."

"This would be a tale of small-town politics if it weren't for the murder," Binder said. "I've seen way worse things happen over a vote in a town meeting."

"If you're talking about someone being shoved, yes, for sure we've seen worse," Flynn said. "Maybe even robbed. But thirty-five thousand dollars? That amount plus the physical attack moved the robbery out of the category of a misdemeanor."

Binder nodded. "Into the category of a felony, which was enough leverage to get both Kirwin and Farrow talking."

"You mean they're not being charged?"

"I didn't say that," Binder said. "They have been charged. Down the road the DA may recommend some leniency if they help us convict Ms. Kirwin."

"Whatever happened to the oyster spat?" I asked.

Binder laughed. "It's in the Great River upwellers. Farrow moved it there the day after Andie died. None of us thought to check."

I remembered Farrow bending over the upwellers that morning. I hadn't realized what he was doing.

"Pinney murdered Andie," I said.

"She'd had enough. Clark had told her about Farrow's campaign against Andie. Clark thought she'd be pleased. But she understood Andie better than either of them did. She knew a robbery wouldn't be enough to end Andie's expansion plans. After it was botched, she took matters into her own hands."

"We interviewed Pinney early on," Flynn said. "We knew from our other interviews there was animosity between her and the victim, but we never took her seriously."

"Because she was an older woman," I said. "But she was strong and determined."

"And she was a scuba diver," Binder added. "It was her tank that blew up the shed."

"The explosion . . ." I had almost forgotten.

"When she hunted Andie, she came and went silently

in that rowboat," Flynn continued. "That meant she had the element of surprise. She killed Andie under the river, loaded her into her rowboat and took her back to the Great River dock to make sure she was found, and the lease hearing was cancelled."

"What about the knife?"

"We think she used it to puncture the line carrying oxygen from Andie's tank. The stab in the neck was an impulse. She may have wished to implicate Mack Owen, just as it appeared. Maybe Ms. Kirwin knew or suspected he inherited, or maybe she hadn't forgiven him for the original purchase of the land."

"Why did I get hit on the head?" I asked.

"Farrow had pretty much figured it out. Once he realized Clark and Mack were innocent, he knew it had to be Pinney and he knew why. He found both the plan and the letter to the trustees in Andie's desk. When he thought he and Mack were going into business together, he called Clark's dad to give him a heads up that he and Mack were interested in proceeding with the deal. Mr. Kirwin wasted no time in calling Pinney and shoving that back in her face. She went to Midden Bay to confront Farrow and found you instead."

"I don't know when she got there. I didn't hear her car. She may have seen me through the living room window putting the documents back on Farrow's worktable. I had it pretty well worked out by then."

"Her plan was to ambush Farrow, so she left her car down on the road. She got you instead, but she still intended to go after him, so she had to get you off his property," Flynn said. "She took you back to The Chandlery and dragged you to the shed."

"She dragged me." No wonder I was so sore.

"She's strong and you're tiny," Flynn said.

"Not tiny," I corrected.

He smiled. "Small, petite, short, whatever."

"And then she was going to burn me." I shivered. "All for one sixth of a house."

"Her one-sixth share of the that house is pretty much the only thing she owns," Binder said. "She lives there year-round."

It had never occurred to me. Just as the fact that she had the strength to kill Andie had never occurred to the detectives. But then I thought about it. The careworn condition of the house. The fact that she never allowed her siblings or cousins to visit. She had to stand guard over The Chandlery all the time. And those clothes, the pastels, the headbands. They could have been bought last year or twenty years ago. But people, even people about to lose their homes, didn't kill. "Pinney's identity and The Chandlery's identity had merged," I said. "She was the house. The house was her. To tear down the house was to obliterate her. So she fought back, intensely and crazily, against her own oblivion."

CHAPTER NINETEEN

They discharged me from the hospital after twenty-four hours. I had bruises and abrasions, nothing worse. They'd tested me and observed me long enough to be sure my head bump was just a head bump.

Mom settled me in my old room, and I slept. Not sure if I was dreaming or awake, I heard people come and go. My sister came with her kids. She and Mom murmured in the kitchen for a long time. Later I heard Sonny in my office having a conversation with a woman. Below my room, the front door opened.

"I'm sorry, Chris. She's sleeping," Mom said.

"Can I go up? I just want to see she's okay."

Long pause. "I don't think that's a good idea."

And then I slept some more.

When it was dark, Mom appeared in my room with a chicken sandwich and ginger ale on a tray. "I can come downstairs," I said. "I'm achy and my head is bumped. I'm not sick."

"You didn't seem in a hurry to come down, so I thought I'd better come to you."

I realized I wasn't in a hurry to come downstairs. Or to get out of bed. And restart my real life. "I need to get a new phone," I said.

"You do." Mom smiled. "But maybe not for a few days."

"I heard Chris at the door."

"He's been back a few times. I wasn't sure if you wanted to see him. Flynn told me you asked him not to call Chris when you were hurt. I didn't know what to do." She hesitated. "Chris said to tell you he's sorry."

Sorry for what, I wondered. Sorry for keeping me out of his life? Sorry for not apologizing sooner? Sorry for not answering my question about whether he wanted me fully in or fully out of his life?

"He seemed very sorry, if that helps," Mom said.

I wasn't sure it did. "I have a decision to make," I said. Chris hadn't sworn to me he'd never keep anything from me again and he'd do anything for us to stay together when he'd had the chance. Perhaps he knew himself too well. It was going to be my decision. Accept him on his terms, as he was, because I did love him. Or demand that he be someone else. "About Chris," I added.

My mother sat on my bed. "I figured."

"What do you think I should do?"

"You haven't told me what the issue is, but I've observed you two as a couple for a long time now. Do you remember the last time I sat at your bedside and gave you advice about love?"

"I do." It has been two and a half years earlier, and the

conversation had taken place at Busman's Harbor Hospital, not in my old room. I had been teetering on the brink of beginning a romance with Chris at the time. "You said you were certain of Dad's love. You craved each other's respect. He loved you as you were, and his love brought out the best parts in you."

Did I love Chris as he was? Did I bring out the best of him? I'd always thought I had, but then the secrets piled upon secrets.

"And?" Mom prompted. The lines over her nose were deeper than I remembered them. No doubt from worry about her older child.

"And trust," I answered. "You trusted him with your life, and with mine and Livvie's."

"I meant I trusted him to protect us if that was necessary. But I also meant I trusted that I knew him, knew how he would react in any situation. I trusted him to be himself, the man I loved, always. Do you trust Chris?"

When I didn't answer, she stood to go. "I'll let you think," she said.

Le Roi ran through the open door and settled on my bed, triumphant.

A week later the clambake opened to paying customers. It was my third opening day as the boss and I didn't have the level of jitters I'd had in previous years. There would be mistakes. I hoped they'd be ones the guests wouldn't notice. Over the summer, things would smooth out and we'd run like a well-oiled machine. At least that was the goal.

We'd had the soft opening, our annual trial run for family and friends, the day before. Uncle Bob and Aunt

Sharon had come, for the first time in years, and they'd recruited my dad's other siblings and their spouses as well. We got caught up on what everyone was doing, their kids, their health, and their jobs. Livvie had come out of the clambake kitchen to greet them all and say hello. Mom had left the gift shop to sit at their table during the meal. "What about your friend Chris?" Aunt Sharon asked. "Is he here?"

My mother had responded with a sharp shake of her head that closed the matter. Aunt Sharon didn't bring it up again.

It was a beautiful day and the clambake restored me, as it always did. It was a joy to see the multi-generational families and groups of old friends. A couple about my age held hands as they came off the *Jacquie II*, and I felt a momentary prick in my chest. I shook it off and got on with the glorious day.

"How's it going?" I asked Sonny, out of earshot of his new employees, Walter, who worked at the high school, and Marty Flanaghan. While I was convalescing, he'd felt bad about how he'd behaved and had contacted her on his own to set up her interview. Maybe it worked out better that way. It wasn't me, telling him what to do.

"They've got a lot to learn," he grunted. I took his pronouncement to be an optimistic thing. If he thought they could learn, then he thought they could stay.

While I'd lain in bed in my childhood room, Sonny, Livvie, and Mom had filled all the clambake's jobs. Except one. I gave the only remaining waitress position to Lacey Brenneman. It was a gamble, but I was certain that, as motivated as she was, away from the influence of Clark Kirwin, she would do a fine job.

After the meal, I walked around the island as I always

did, making sure no guest got left behind. When I reached Windsholme, I ducked inside. I went up to my future apartment and stood at the window over my future kitchen sink.

Two days before, at the marina, I'd approached Chris's sailboat *The Dark Lady*. "Permission to come aboard."

He'd popped up out of the hatch. "This is a surprise."

I'd boarded the boat and sat on a bench at the stern. He sat kitty corner to me, almost knee to knee, but not quite touching. The sun was bright, and I was squinting.

"I called like a hundred times," he said. "I tried to come and see you but your mom—"

"I know." I paused to make sure I had his attention. I took a deep breath and said as quickly as I could, "I've come to tell you it's over. I'm sorry I gave you an ultimatum. That wasn't the way to handle it. But I've decided I can't go on as we are."

He stared at the deck. "I'm sorry. I'm sorry I didn't tell you about my family when we first got together. I'm sorry I didn't introduce you to my friends. I regret—all of it. I've been happier with you than I have ever been in my life." He stopped. "I don't know why I couldn't do what I should have."

I almost melted then. I did love him. But I couldn't worry about what was around the next corner. Ming was right. He wasn't ashamed of me. Deep inside him there was a pit of shame. I had strong inklings of what had caused it, but I didn't know the whole story. Until he was ready to tell me, we couldn't be together. I wasn't sure he would ever be.

"Come and get your stuff anytime." Tears sprang to my eyes. It's amazing how you can bulldog your way through the big stuff, only to have something unimportant like the logistics get to you. Because that would make it real. His clothes gone from the closet, his shaving stuff from the bathroom.

We stood and he held me close. I felt his strong chest, maybe for the last time. Probably for the last time. And then I walked away.

Down at the dock, Captain George blew the whistle on the *Jacquie II* and the guests gathered their things to board the boat. I took one last look around my apartment-to-be. "Living here is going to be great," I said out loud.

Then I ran down the stairs and to the dock to catch the boat. The season had begun.

RECIPES

Oyster Stuffing

This isn't a Thanksgiving book, but it is an oyster book and I couldn't resist the impulse to include this amazing stuffing. In the book, Julia's Aunt Sharon is famous for making this stuffing. In real life, my husband made it "as an experiment" for our enormous family Thanksgiving celebration along with our more traditional recipe. The oyster stuffing was gone in a flash with everyone clamoring for more.

Ingredients

8 cups cornbread in ½-inch cubes
1 Tablespoon canola oil
4 ounces pancetta
8 ounces andouille sausage meat removed from casings
3 Tablespoons butter
2 medium yellow onions, chopped
1 cup celery chopped
½ Tablespoon dried sage
½ teaspoon salt
½ teaspoon ground black pepper
1 cup chicken stock
1 pint shucked oysters, drained and chopped

Instructions

Pre-heat oven to 350 degrees.
Grease a 2-quart casserole with butter.
Put cornbread cubes in large bowl.
Heat the canola oil in a 10-inch pan and add the pan-

cetta. Cook until the pancetta browns and remove from pan.

Add the sausage meat to the pan and brown, stirring to break up any large pieces. Remove to same container as pancetta.

Melt the butter in the pan and add the onions, celery, sage, salt, and pepper. Sauté for 5 minutes.

Add the chicken stock and return the pancetta and sausage to the pan. Cook together for 5 minutes. Pour over the cornbread stirring constantly to break up the cubes.

Fold in the oysters.

Put in the casserole dish and bake for 45-50 minutes, or until the top begins to turn brown.

Serves 8 to 12 as a side dish.

Banana Bread

This is my late mother-in-law's recipe for banana bread. She never really adjusted when all her kids grew up and moved out. She shopped until she died for a family of eight. As a result, she always had way too many bananas to consume before they went soft, and therefore she almost always had banana bread on hand when her grandkids came to visit her. They loved the banana bread and I love that they still make it according to her recipe.

Ingredients

½ cup butter
1 cup sugar
2 eggs beaten lightly
1 cup mashed bananas (3 large, ripe)
1½ Tablespoons light cream
1 teaspoon lemon juice
2 cups sifted flour
1½ teaspoons baking powder
¼ teaspoon salt
½ teaspoon baking soda
1 cup chopped pecans or walnuts

Instructions

Cream butter and sugar and add eggs. Add cream and lemon juice to mashed bananas and combine with the butter, sugar, and eggs. Add sifted flour, baking powder, baking soda and salt, and finally the nuts. Stir only enough to blend. Bake in a greased loaf pan at 350 degrees for 45 minutes.

Serves 6 to 10.

Baked Oysters

For those who, like Julia, are reluctant to eat raw oysters, this recipe combines some of the elements of a classic mignonette with cheese for a tangy oyster experience.

Ingredients

12-16 oysters, shucked, drained, put back in the shell,
    and laid out on a baking sheet
4 ounces cream cheese, softened
2 Tablespoons sour cream
1 small or ½ large shallot
1 jalapeño pepper, seeds removed and finely minced
1 teaspoon wine vinegar
¼ teaspoon freshly cracked black pepper
¼ cup shredded cheddar cheese
grated parmesan cheese

Instructions

Pre-heat oven to 450 degrees.

Stir together the cream cheese, sour cream, shallot, jalapeno, wine vinegar, and cracked pepper. Fold in the shredded cheddar.

Put a heaping teaspoon of the cheese mixture on top of each oyster to cover.

Sprinkle with parmesan cheese.

Bake 8-10 minutes until cheese melts.

Serve immediately. Serves 3 to 4.

Sous Vide Spicy Tuna

This dish is served at Mack's Shack as a small plate, but it can also be an entree. It tastes absolutely delicious and is gorgeous to look at with the pink color of the tuna and the green of the cucumber and cilantro. This is a great choice for people who love tuna but prefer not to eat it raw.

Ingredients

For the Tuna:

8 ounces fresh tuna cut $1\frac{1}{2}$ to 2 inches thick
2 Tablespoons Sriracha
1 Tablespoon sesame oil
3 scallions, sliced

For the Fixings:

cooked sushi rice
1 avocado, sliced
1 cucumber, peeled, quartered, and diced
2-3 Tablespoons white sesame seeds, toasted
Sriracha mayonnaise
1 jalapeno pepper, seeded and diced
$\frac{1}{2}$ cup chopped cilantro

Instructions

Generously salt the tuna on all sides and seal in a zippered plastic bag. Allow to rest in the fridge for at least 30 minutes.

Pre-heat the water bath to 105 degrees according to your sous vide instructions.

Stir Sriracha and sesame oil together. When water bath is ready, remove the tuna from the bag and brush liberally with half this mixture.

Return the tuna to the bag and seal, leaving a small opening at the corner. Gently lower the bag into the water bath, allowing the water to push any remaining air out through the corner of the bag before sealing completely.

Cook the tuna for 45-60 minutes depending on thickness. Remove from the bag and cool for ten minutes. Slice and cut tuna into medium dice. Mix with remaining Sriracha and sesame oil, and half the scallions. Put in fridge for 15 minutes.

Put rice on plate. Top with avocado, cucumber, cooled tuna, and sesame seeds. Drizzle with mayonnaise. Pass the jalapeno, remaining scallions, and cilantro.

Serves 2 to 4.

Lobster Mashed Potatoes

These mashed potatoes are a huge hit at Mack's "time" for Andie. They were served as an appetizer in a martini glass, garnished with a green olive. They can also be served as side dish.

Ingredients

4 russet potatoes
2 cups lobster stock
8 Tablespoons butter, divided
2 large shallots, chopped
¼ cup heavy cream
12 ounces cooked lobster meat, roughly chopped
salt and pepper to taste
snipped chives for garnish
green olive stuffed with pimento for garnish

Instructions

Peel the potatoes and place in a pot of water to cover by 2 inches. Bring to a boil and simmer for 10 minutes. Drain and set aside to cool. Cut into cubes.

Heat the lobster stock in a small saucepan.

Melt half the butter in a large sauté pan and add the shallots. Sauté for 3 minutes.

Add the potatoes and heat for one minute. Begin adding ladlefuls of stock one at a time, stirring until absorbed by the potatoes, before adding the next until the stock is depleted. Stir in the cream and continue cooking until mostly absorbed. Add remaining butter and season with salt and pepper.

Mash the potato mixture. Gently fold in the cooked lobster meat.

Place in 6 to 8 martini glasses. Garnish with chives and green olive.

Acknowledgments

I've loved the town of Damariscotta, Maine, for a long time. It has a great main street for shopping and dining, terrific art galleries, a fabulous library, and a wonderful bookstore. It has a unique and intriguing name of disputed origins, huge piles of oyster shells left by ancient Americans, a festival in the spring where the alewives are cheered as they climb fish ladders to move from the salty water of the river to the fresh water of Damariscotta Lake to spawn (really) and a Pumpkinfest in the fall with the most amazing decorated pumpkins you've ever seen. Damariscotta is also the gateway to the Pemaquid Peninsula where you'll find the beautiful Pemaquid Lighthouse, a colonial fort, and a wonderful little beach. You should go there. Really.

And it also has oyster farms. Five of them. What the Damariscotta River doesn't have is a Great River Oyster Farm, or a Midden Bay Oyster Farm. I made those up. It also doesn't have people murdering one another. I made that up, too.

I first learned about the oyster farms on the fabulous Damariscotta River Cruises, a narrated tour of the wildlife, history, and oyster farms on the river, along with an oyster tasting. My family and friends have spent many happy hours on the tour.

Thank you to Glidden Point Oysters for the tour of the farm and for answering my many eager questions. Sorry for creating the two extra competitors. And, of course, the body. All mistakes both deliberate and inadvertent are my own.

For those whose interest in oyster farming has been piqued by this novel, I recommend the following books. *Shucked: Life on a New England Oyster Farm*, by Erin Byers Murray, a memoir by a woman who upended her professional and personal life so she could work on an oyster farm in Duxbury, Massachusetts. This was the perfect book for someone like me who had only the vaguest notions about the subject. Murray takes you right along with her as she learns the business. *The Oyster War: The True Story of a Small Farm, Big Politics, and the future of Wilderness in America* tells the story of a battle over the expansion of an oyster farm in northern California. The book is about a different breed of oyster and a different kind of farming than is practiced in Maine, but the book also contains a long and fascinating history of oyster farming in the United States. *The Geography of Oysters: The Connoisseur's Guide to Oyster Eating in North America* offers a delicious explanation of the interplay of nature and nurture on the taste, texture, and size of the various oysters found in North America.

Thanks to the Moore family at the real Cabbage Island Clambake, who put up with all the murder and mayhem I have created. You should definitely visit them if you are ever in Boothbay Harbor, Maine. In fact, you should go to Boothbay Harbor, Maine, explicitly to visit them.

Thank you to my husband, Bill Carito, who developed all the recipes in the book except the banana bread, which was his mother's. He never misses his deadlines, even as I careen toward my own.

I would like to thank, as always, the team at Kensington Books, especially my editor, John Scognamiglio, and my publicist, Larissa Ackerman. They have both gone above and beyond to support me and the Maine Clambake Mystery series.

A special shout out to my Wicked Authors, Sherry Harris, Jessica Ellicott, Maddie Day, Cate Conte, and Julia Henry. I don't know what I would do without you, but I do know my life would be sadly diminished. Special thanks go out to Jessica who spent a chilly day at her dining room table in Old Orchard Beach, Maine, working on the story. And to Sherry, who always finds time to read my manuscripts and give me such valuable comments.

And thank you, with great love, to my family, who put up with my absences to attend conferences, my culling their lives and photos for blog posts, and my long days in "book jail." I love you, Bill Carito, Rob, Sunny and Viola Carito, and Kate, Luke, Etta, and Sylvie Donius.

Grab These Cozy Mysteries
from
Kensington Books